QUIRKY

THE COMPLETE
Q COLLECTION

AN ANTHOLOGY OF QUICKIES

JENNIE KEW

QUIRKY: THE COMPLETE Q COLLECTION

ISBN: 978-0-6451076-8-5

Copyright © 2022 by Jennie Kew
Published by Wooden Key Press
Edited by Hot Tree Editing
Cover design by Wooden Key Press

www.jenniekew.com

Praise for Jennie's books

The Viking Blues – Heart Award 2021 (2022)
Erotic Romance – Winner

The Viking Blues – Passionate Plume Award 2022
Short Contemporary Romance – Finalist

The Viking Blues – Stiletto Award 2022
Erotic Romance – Finalist

His Own Heaven – Passionate Plume Award 2021
BDSM Romance – Winner

His Own Heaven – Stiletto Award 2021
Long Romance – Finalist

This Time Around – Koru Award of Excellence 2020
Short Romance – 2nd Place

This Time Around – Stiletto Award 2020
Mid-length Romance – Finalist

Third Time Lucky – Passionate Plume Award 2019
BDSM Romance – Finalist

Third Time Lucky – Stiletto Award 2019
Erotic/BDSM Romance – Finalist

"The characters will pull on your heart strings and leave you breathless."
Review for *Revenge and Redemption*

"The chemistry between the hero and heroine is incredible."
Review for *Sacrifice and Seduction*

NO REST FOR THE WICKED

For Dan, my very own devil-in-disguise.

No Rest for the Wicked

Ever wonder why men fall asleep after sex? Because shooting our load releases a shit-ton of a groovy little hormone called prolactin. Sure, it mixes with a couple of other hormones to make for the best go-sleepy-bye cocktail ever, but mostly it's the prolactin.

Now, for human males, sex isn't vital for sleep. Hell, overindulging on burgers and beer is enough to knock out their lightweight arses. But for an incubus? Well, we sex demons need our prolactin cocktails like most creatures need air to breathe. Without sex, we don't sleep a wink.

And I haven't had sex in over a year.

Fuck, I'm tired.

"Hey, boss? You awake?"

My assistant, Bianca, nudges my shoulder, hands me my second triple espresso of the evening then neatly places a stack of papers on the desk in front of me. I stiffen as she brushes against me—in more places than one. Was that her soft breast I felt against my shoulder? No. Of course not. My sleep-deprived brain is playing tricks on me again.

I blink my weary eyes at the paper, at the line after line

of nonsensical gibberish she's forcing me to look at. "What are these?"

She hands me my reading glasses. "Résumés for the head bartender job." She's all business. "Rob leaves for Europe in two weeks. You can't put this off any longer."

I stare at the glasses in her outstretched hand. *Stupid human body.* In my true form, I am a specimen of physical perfection—tall, healthy, virile, 20/10 vision. In my human form... shit, I'm *still* a specimen of physical perfection, but having to disguise my demon eyes means my eyesight sucks.

Bianca stares at me like I'm dense and waves the glasses under my nose. Taking them—and resisting the urge to throw them out the window—I wonder how she'd react if I showed her what I truly look like, without the stupid fucking glasses or this ridiculous human façade?

As demons go, incubi are pretty standard fare. Red skin, horns, tail, cloven feet, 8-pack abs and a porn-worthy cock. But unlike most of demonkind, incubi are blessed with pretty faces too. So pretty in fact that many of my incubi brethren are models here in the human realm. No, not the fashion show–type models. With their crappy vision, they'd walk right off the end of the runway. But the hot guys you see in those fancy eyewear commercials?

Yeah. They're demons.

With a sigh, I slide the glasses up my nose and then reach for my coffee. The hot, bitter deliciousness slides down my throat, and it takes but a moment for the extra-strong caffeine to take effect. My mind clears, focuses.

Résumés. Bartender. Check.

But before I begin, I cast one last lingering glance in Bianca's direction and catch her adjusting her bra strap. I watch her slide her delicate fingers under the neckline of her shirt to fidget with the strap holding up her bountiful breasts. My fingers twitch, eager to reach out and touch her, to feel the silkiness of her skin, the heat of her body. The fullness of her curves.

A few months back, my insomnia made me stupid, made me forget to bite my tongue when she leaned over my desk and gave me a front row ticket to the best show in town. Staring directly down her cleavage, I'd blurted out, "Fuck, you have great tits."

Not exactly Shakespeare, I know, but instead of crying or quitting or threatening to sue for sexual harassment, she'd laughed, and then she'd grinned and said, "Don't get too excited. It's just a really good bra."

I've been dying to test that theory ever since.

Bianca shrugs as if she's still uncomfortable, but stops fidgeting and straightens her collar. She's wearing a blouse today instead of her usual T-shirt. Pale pink with little black skulls printed all over it and silver skull buttons. Paired with tight, black arse-hugging jeans and purple biker boots and she looks metal as fuck! So goddamn sexy.

I always love the way Bianca dresses, but I thank God especially on days like today. Yes, God. He created these wondrous beings, after all. Gave them tits. Hey, every guy has his favourite body part, okay, and I know it probably seems like I'm obsessed with Bianca's breasts, but that's only because I am. Why? Because her double-Ds fill out that blouse to the point I fear—*hope*—the buttons will burst, and they'll spill out into the open and—

Straightening in my chair, I clear my throat. I don't have time to daydream.

Résumés. Bartender.... *So tired.*

I'm Rugaal, by the way, or Ryan as I'm known here in the human realm, and this is my nightclub, Grind. My office is conveniently located above the main-floor bathrooms, with a large glass window overlooking the dance floor, bar and lounges.

I say convenient because, as an incubus, especially one who's not currently getting any, I require the people around me to have sex instead, and you'd be surprised how many people get laid in nightclub bathrooms.

Every time someone gets some, and I mean everything from heavy petting to full-on down-and-dirty bumping uglies, a buttload of sexual energy is released into the ether, and if an incubus just happens to be nearby, thanks for the snack. And while devouring the sexual energy of others doesn't feed me anywhere close to what I need, it's enough to keep me alive.

Tired—and always just a little bit hungry—but alive.

So why don't I just have sex with someone and get a good night's sleep?

Because thirteen months ago, I met Bianca.

I remember the first time I saw her like it was yesterday. Dressed in blue jeans, combat boots and a faded Hellboy T-shirt that lovingly embraced her magnificent breasts, she'd walked into my office and set up shop in my heart. And then she'd sat down and told me exactly how she was going to help me make my club a success.

Every word out of her mouth had me mesmerised, not that I'd heard a word of it. Honestly, the woman could have told me the Sydney Opera House was made of Swiss cheese and I'd have happily nodded along in agreement. I'd been too distracted by the once-in-a-lifetime event happening before my eyes to do anything other than stare at her in wonder.

My brothers had warned me this would happen, that I would succumb to the need only our beloved could inspire in us, and not wanting to lose her, I'd hired her on the spot.

It was only after she'd exited the building and my faculties had sufficiently returned to normal that I'd bothered to read her resume. Thankfully her letters of recommendation had shone brighter than an angel's arse at Christmas, and over the past year we'd become quite the team, professionally speaking.

And therein lies my problem.

The last thing I want right now is a professional relationship with Bianca. I'm in love with her. And not just any old kind of love but head-over-fucking-heels in love. With my assistant. My beautiful, gracious, clever, nerdy, tough-as-nails assistant.

But here's the thing about being an incubus in love: I can't get it up for any other woman in the world. No one. Nada. Not happening.

Believe me, I've tried.

I can get it up for her, though, as the tent pole in my pants is currently demonstrating, but the sad truth is Bianca is the best damned assistant I've ever had, and as much as I crave the taste of her pussy in my mouth, the smell of her sweat-slicked breasts in my nostrils and the feel of her soft, plump body in my hands, I won't risk losing her.

I can't.

I try to focus on the work in front of me, but the words all blur together. I can't concentrate. I can't sit still. Lurching out of my chair, I pace my office. For over a year I've kept my feelings—and my hands—to myself. If only she'd make the first move. But I know she never will. Her work ethics prevent her from sleeping with the boss. Besides the "great tits" incident, she's never even flirted with me.

I stop pacing and stare at her through the glass wall that separates my office from her desk in the reception area. Her fingers fly over the keyboard of her computer, her fingernails painted black. The phone rings, she answers it, quick and professional, and then she leans forward and bops the nose on the limited-edition Batman bobblehead that sits on her desk, the one I bought for her last month, for our one year anniversary. I'd caught her drooling over an advertisement for it in the back of a comic book and knew she had to have it. One corner of her mouth lifts in a lopsided grin as she watches the head bounce around.

I want her.

Most men overlook Bianca, see only the nerdy girl, or the insignificant secretary, or the pudgy girl not worthy of their time. They sneer at her soft body, at the muffin-top that sits above her jeans, and poke fun at her "childish" hobbies.

They don't see what I see.

They don't take the time to see the intelligence shining in her lovely eyes, or the humour that constantly clings to her sultry mouth, lifting one corner of her lips in a smirk that haunts my lonely, waking hours. And as for that muffin-top, that smooth, pale patch of flesh that taunts me with what I can't have, it's almost as maddening as her cleavage, tempting me to grab her hips and pull her body into mine so I can grind my erection against her soft arse.

I know my exhaustion is riding me hard, but that's not why I want to fuck her. At this point, a decent night's sleep would simply be the cherry on top.

I ache for her.

I long for her touch, to feel her hands on me, her mouth on me, her tantalising voice close by my ear. I want to know how it feels to be inside her tight, wet pussy, to feel the rocking of her hips as she straddles my lap and fucks me slowly, to feel my balls slap against her thighs as I take her from behind and fuck her like a wild beast.

And, who knows? Maybe she'd be into it, fucking a demon. All those comic books she reads have to count for something, don't they? Don't they prove she's already a little left of centre?

I need to calm down. I need to remember all the reasons why fucking her is a bad idea. And I need to ignore the crushing of my heart and swallow down the disappointment and regret I feel every time I convince myself to look away from her.

Taking my seat, I try to focus.

Résumés. Bartender....

Fuck it.

She's worth the risk.

"Bianca!" Impatience makes me ignore the intercom at the side of my desk and I simply yell her name instead. She holds up a finger to signal she'll be another moment. My palms sweat. I'm nervous. I'm a fucking demon, and this human woman makes me nervous. But then, I am about to ask her to let me fuck her every which way come Sunday for the rest of her natural life. Removing my glasses, I pinch the bridge of my nose, will away the tension coiling itself around my skull.

A moment later, she pushes the door open just far enough to stick her head through the gap, but doesn't come in. "Yes?"

I motion for her to enter and take a seat, then I stand and pace once more.

Her brow furrows as she watches me. "I'm cutting you off," she says in a tone that brooks no opposition. "No more espressos for you or you'll never get any sleep."

I laugh at the very real possibility of being awake for an eternity, although it has nothing to do with caffeine. Then I see the direction of her gaze drift south until she's staring directly at my erection, eyes wide, jaw slack, blatantly ogling. A flash of triumph flickers along my veins as I watch her swallow hard.

My beloved likes what she sees.

The tip of her tongue sweeps over her lips, desire flashes through her expression, and it heats me all the way through to my core.

I burn for her.

Her gaze still focused on my cock, she says, "The club opens in fifteen minutes. Did you want something in particular?"

"Yes."

"What?"

"You."

Her head snaps up, her gaze meets mine. Her expression one of bewildered hope. "Me?"

"Yes, beloved. I want you."

Bianca stares at me as though she's never noticed before that I'm six feet and five inches of well-muscled male. Or maybe she has. The suddenly sultry look in her eyes as they meet mine says she's noticed a lot of things before tonight, and that's when it hits me.

I'm not the only one around here pretending to be something I'm not.

A hot-blooded vixen has been hiding behind the exterior of my cool, calm and capable assistant. Her expression turns shrewd. "You want me for... what, exactly?"

I groan. "You're not going to make this easy for me, are you?"

Her lips curve into a seductive little smile. "Nope."

I pause for a moment, unsure how to proceed. Normally as soon as a woman realises I want to fuck them, they simply throw themselves at me, but nothing about this situation is going to be simple.

And Bianca makes a good point. What, *exactly*, do I want from her? Sex obviously, but what else? My pulse races as the answer screams inside my head, in my heart.

I want her to know I'm an incubus, to touch my demonic body, to skate her delicate fingers over my hot flesh. I want her to know what I taste like, fire and heat and sex and love, to see my horns and tail and hooves and not be afraid of me.

I want her to want me.

Rugaal, not Ryan.

Demon, not human.

I want her to love *me*.

I swallow hard. "I want you to be your usual calm self. And lock the door while I pull the shades."

With the door locked and the windows darkened, I feel more confident. I am a demon, after all. We prefer the shadows. Downstairs I hear the DJ fire up the music. Loud, thumping, sexual.

Perfect.

Bianca sits down again and watches as I pull my shirt free of my jeans. Her gaze is less carnal than before, more curious, as though she's not quite sure if I've lost my mind but she's dying to find out. At least she's not afraid of me.

Not yet.

Exhaustion makes me fumble the buttons on my shirt. Frustrated, I rip it apart.

Eyes wide again, she laughs. "Want some help, boss?"

"Yes."

"What would you do without me?" Standing, she comes to me and plucks the tattered remnants of my shirt from my pants, strips them off my arms and drops them to the floor.

Her hands brush against my sides, and she recoils, burned. "Your skin is so hot."

That curious light fills her gaze again. She presses her fingertips against my abdomen. I suck in a breath. Her cool fingers against my heat feel heavenly. Sliding her palms over my naked chest, they graze across my nipples and I shudder with delight.

"Are you always this hot?" She's standing so close I can feel her breath brush over my skin when she speaks.

"No, not always."

"But—"

I press a finger to her lips and silence her. "I have simply denied myself for too long, denied my need for your soothing touch." She frowns at my words, her expression questioning. "All will be revealed soon enough. Please, trust me."

Her brow smoothing out, Bianca smiles and nods. I drop my hands to my waist and unfasten my belt buckle. She watches as I unzip my pants, gasps when my cock springs free of its confinement. But when she reaches out and wraps her hands around my hard length, I'm the one that gasps. Her soft palm against my flesh feels so damn good.

"I always knew you'd be big, but holy fuck."

I laugh. I can't help it. Knowing she's thought about me naked makes me happy, and the look of wonder on her face as she handles my cock with such reverence is amusing to me. I can't wait to see her reaction once she knows my true size. Can't wait to hear her screams of ecstasy when I fuck her senseless.

I settle her back in the chair, then toe off my shoes and kick off my pants, remove my watch and set it on my desk. I stand before her in all my glory, every inch of the human she has come to know on display for her, but I'm not exactly naked. Not yet. Her tongue sweeps over her lips again and I long to taste it. To taste her.

"I want you to see me."

Her gaze dances over the full length of my body and back again. "I can see you. Quite a lot of you."

I'm nervous again and wring my hands. "No. I need you to see the *real* me. Please, beloved. Don't be afraid."

Her brow furrows the way it always does when she questions my sanity. "Okay."

I shake out my fingers and try to relax, close my eyes and concentrate. I slow my heart, my breathing, and meditate.

My façade slips away and Bianca gasps as I begin to change.

My feet morph into hooves and add six inches to my height. My short-cropped hair lengthens until it flows down my back, the colour changing from brown to black. My muscles expand, my biceps, my thighs, everything becoming more defined, more rigid, and my skin takes on its natural blood-red hue.

Horns grow slowly from the sides of my head, curling and twisting much like a ram's. My cock thickens, lengthens, and my balls grow heavy with my inexorable need to bond with her, to claim her as mine.

Finally, my—

"Holy shit! You have a tail?"

My eyes pop open as I feel Bianca's cool touch at the base of my spine, her fingers gliding along the length of my tail as it grows to its full extent. My heart stutters in my chest.

She's not afraid of me.

Glancing over my shoulder, I grin at the look of sheer

amazement on her face. Turning, I take her hands in mine, answer the question I see burning in her gaze.

"I'm an incubus."

Her brow creases in thought. "Incubus? That's a sex demon, right?"

I stroke my fingers down the side of her face, touching her the way I've longed to for months. "Yes."

"But... how? I thought demons were a myth," she says as she ducks under my arm and continues exploring my body. "And if demons are real, then—holy shit! That does mean God is real too?"

I grin at her curiosity. "Yes."

"Wow. I should really go to church more," she mutters under her breath, then looks up at me with one brow raised. "So if you're a sex demon—"

"Incubus."

"Incubus, right. And you're revealing yourself to me, I guess that means you want to fuck me, huh?"

My grin grows indulgent at her questions, her curiosity. "Yes."

She reaches up and presses her hand against my cheek. I lean into her touch and close my eyes, savouring the feel of her soft skin.

Until she slaps me. "It's about damn time!"

Wait. "What?"

She anchors her hands on her hips. "When you told me I had great tits, I thought I'd *finally* gotten your attention, but then... nothing! Not only have you never mentioned them again, but you freeze every time I get close to you. In the end, I just put the whole thing down to a slip of the tongue because you were going through caffeine withdrawal."

I snort. "I freeze whenever you're close because it's the

only way I can stop myself from tearing your clothes off and screwing you on whatever flat surface is close at hand. And it wasn't caffeine I was lacking. It was sleep. Why do you think I mainline the triple espressos in the first place?"

Her brow creases. "You have insomnia?"

"Insomnia would be an improvement. Bianca, I haven't slept since I met you."

She rolls her eyes at me. "Exaggerate much?"

"No. Really." I give her a quick lesson in demonology.

Her mouth hangs slack. "So, you haven't slept at all?"

I fold my arms across my chest. "Nope."

"Because you want me?"

"Because I want *only* you."

She stares at me with a look of sheer bewilderment, as if she needs a moment to absorb my words, but then she squares her shoulders and lifts her chin, her expression one of resolve. "All right then."

Bianca unzips her jeans and shoves them down her thighs, and for a moment I'm too distracted by the white lacy panties she's wearing to question her actions. My mind clears when she sits down to unlace her boots, hiding the sexy scrap of lace from my sight.

"What are you doing? Stop."

Still bent forward, her hands cease pulling at the laces and she looks up at me. "No. I'm not letting you stay awake another minute longer than you need to. If it's my fault you haven't slept in all this time, then it's my responsibility to fix this."

"I'm not talking about that."

"Then what?"

I crouch before her and take her boot in my hands. "I wanted to undress you myself."

"Oh." She blushes, and it's the cutest thing I think I've

ever seen. My confident, efficient assistant, so used to doing what needs to be done before I even ask that she didn't even consider that I might want to get her naked with my own two hands.

I slip her boot off her foot and begin unlacing the other. "And my lack of sleep isn't your fault. I should've had the guts to do this sooner."

She tilts her head to one side and studies me. "Why didn't you?"

I remove her other boot and bid her stand. "I didn't want to be a cliché. The sleazy boss hitting on his secretary."

She lifts her chin. "Executive assistant."

"Executive assistant. I didn't want you to quit."

Cocking one brow, she says, "You thought I'd quit if you fucked me? That doesn't bode well for the rest of the evening."

She's teasing me. I'm a seven-foot-tall, blood-red monster from the depths of hell, and she's teasing me.

My chest swells with pride and my cock twitches with anticipation.

I make short work of her jeans and panties, sliding them down her long legs and adding them to the growing pile of clothes on the floor. I skim my hands over her voluptuous hips, and she trembles under my touch, but before I can stand, she tunnels her fingers through my hair. I look up at her, at the heated expression lighting her face.

"Please."

She speaks so softly I barely hear the word, but I am compelled to obey. I slide my hands down her thighs and lift one leg, supporting her weight and opening her up to my touch. She's so wet.

Slipping my fingers between her legs, I press deeper between her folds. She quivers with every slow, calculated thrust and her ragged breaths match my rhythm. The heat of her sex rivals that of my own skin, and the strength of her pussy as she clamps down on my fingers excites me. Imagining how she'll feel wrapped around my thick cock makes my balls tighten with need.

I want to fuck her. Here. Now. But the look of hunger in her eyes as she stares down at me stills the thought. I will fuck her. Hard. But first I will earn that right. First I will pleasure her in every way she desires.

I allow her to guide my head forward until my face is so close to her pussy I can almost taste her. And then I turn my head and press my lips to her leg. It's my turn to tease.

Her skin twitches with every kiss, every nip of my teeth, every lash of my tongue. I work my way down her soft, fleshy inner thigh, away from where she wants me.

She whimpers.

I grin.

Her fingers tighten in my hair, and I take mercy, running my tongue the length of her leg, from the sensitive spot at the back of her knee to the bundle of nerves above her pussy, and then I latch my lips around her clit and suck. Hard.

Moaning loudly, Bianca releases my hair and grabs my horns, pulling me tighter against her, fucking my face. And I devour her cunt like a starving man at a banquet.

Crying out as she succumbs to her passion, her hips jerk and her thighs twitch, and I taste her liquid heat pour across my tongue, feel it drip down my hand.

"Fuck me, Ryan." Her voice is a ragged plea.

"My name isn't Ryan." Climbing to my feet, I stare down at her, square my shoulders and lift my chin, proud of my incubi heritage. "My name is Rugaal, third son of Somaal and his beloved, Amelia."

"Rugaal." My name slips off her tongue like honey. She slides her hands over my chest and presses her body to mine. "Fuck me, Rugaal."

Moving her back until she bumps against my desk, her arse teeters on the edge of the timber and her toes barely touch the floor. I spread her thighs and settle myself between them.

My cock juts up between us, hard and proud and ready, and Bianca rakes her fingernails along its length. Shuddering with need, I want to plunge deep inside her and seal our bond, but I must wait and give her the choice. If she wants me, I'm hers. If not....

I shove the unwanted thought away.

I begin removing her blouse, focusing on each button and resisting the urge to rip the pale pink cotton from her body. "I want you, Bianca. I want to fuck you every way I know how and believe me when I tell you I know. Every. Way. How. And contrary to what you may believe, sleep is *not* my only reason for wanting you."

"It's not?" She brushes her fingertips over my nipples, gently tugs at them until I bite my lip and stifle a moan.

"No, it's not." I slip her blouse from her shoulders and reveal her big, soft breasts. Her bra is made of the same white lace as her panties and her hardened nipples strain against the fabric. I stroke my thumbs over the mountains of flesh exposed above the cups. A pearl of moisture leaks from my cock. Here goes nothing. "I want to bond with you."

She gazes up at me, a slight frown pulling at her features. "Bond?"

"It is similar to a human marriage, only once it is done, it cannot be undone."

She leans forward and licks the valley between my pecs, then continues up to the hollow of my throat. She's driving me crazy, every flick of her tongue pushing my need for her higher. She stares at my chest, her gaze shuttered, unreadable. "Why would you want to bond with me?"

I lift her chin so she can't look away. "Because I've loved you from the moment you walked through my door."

Her eyes widen, her pupils dilate. She looks so uncertain, as though she's not quite sure she believes me. "How do we bond?"

"We fuck. As human and incubus."

I hold very still, my jaw tight and my chin lifted, readying myself for rejection. Sex is one thing, bonding another. It's a lot to ask of a woman who until tonight thought she meant nothing to me.

She reaches up and cups my cheek. Her head is tilted to one side, her eyes narrowed slightly. "What if I want to fuck but don't want to bond? I mean, I did promise to help you get some sleep, after all. And the thought of walking away now seems like a wasted opportunity."

My fingers tighten on her hips and I swallow down my disappointment. Of course she'd come at this as a problem to be solved. That's what she does, my ever-proficient assistant. My throat constricts. My voice dulls. "My human façade prevents the bonding."

Her brow shoots up and her lips twist. "Like a supernatural condom?"

There is humour in her tone. A lot of it. My eyes narrow. "You're teasing me again."

Bianca bursts out laughing and taps my cheek with gentle fingers. "After what you've put us through, you deserve a little teasing. And if we're to be married, you're going to have to get used to my twisted sense of humour."

"You accept the bond?" A wave of relief washes over me.

She strokes her hand down my chest. "Of course I do. You weren't the only one suffering restless nights over this, you know?" At my frown, she adds, "I love you."

My heart stutters in my chest, hardly able to believe the sweet words tumbling from her lips. "And the fact I'm not human really doesn't bother you?"

She smiles and shakes her head. "You should know me better than that by now. And you're still you, aren't you? A bigger, redder, hornier version of you, but... still *you?*"

I lean my forehead against hers, revel in her acceptance. "Yes. I am still me."

She walks her fingers up my chest, tangles them in my hair once more. "Still the man I have wildly inappropriate thoughts about."

I grin. "How inappropriate?"

Her teeth sink into that lush bottom lip of hers, staining it red. "A lot more inappropriate now I know you have a tail."

My grin widens. "Is that so?" Pulling back slightly, I create a gap between us, wide enough to feel the air brush across the fronts of my thighs. Wide enough to fit the tip of my tail.

Threading the long, slender appendage through the gap, I tease her with it, stroke it over her belly, her clit, lower. And then I watch as inch after inch disappears inside her wet and willing pussy.

I marvel at the length she's able to take with seeming ease, revel in the unabashedly wanton sounds spilling from her pretty mouth. A mouth I am yet to taste. "Was this what you had in mind, beloved?"

A stream of nearly unintelligible babble escapes her, but somewhere in there I hear her say, "Yes," and, "Oh my fucking God."

Her hands grip the edge of my desk, and her pelvis flexes, working my tail deep with every thrust. I pull her forward just enough so I can reach behind her and unfasten her bra. The instant the clasp releases, the straps pull free of her shoulders, the weight of her breasts dragging the garment down her body. She grabs the clothing and tugs it free, tossing it away and revealing her beautiful tits in all their magnificence.

I take my erection in one hand, her breast in the other. My tail keeps working her pussy. I rub my thumb over the head of my cock, can't wait to be enveloped by her slick heat. My balls tighten. It won't take much to make me come, not after such abstinence.

Her breast feels heavy in my hand. Heavy and warm and soft. She covers my hand with her own, encouraging me to squeeze her harder, and when she takes her other breast in hand and matches my rhythm, tugs at her nipple and moans, I stroke myself harder, faster. Watching Bianca getting off on my demonic body arouses me like nothing ever has.

Or ever will again.

When she comes, she screams and her whole body spasms. Her pussy is gripping my tail, squeezing it, sending shockwaves of sensation shooting along its length and back up my spine, making my cock jerk in my hand.

Her hand tightens over mine, squashing her breast. My other hand strangles my cock, and I can't hold back. I come, shooting my load all over her breasts, jerking until there's nothing left, and then she draws her fingers through my cream and sucks them into her mouth. My nostrils flare, and I growl my approval at the salacious display.

My woman is as dirty as me.

The thought emboldens me, bolsters my flagging cock with renewed life.

Sleep feathers the edges of my reality, but just like every other time I jerk off, it's the difference between a light snack and a full meal, teasing me with what could be, and I am nowhere near satisfied.

I'm horny as hell, and I'm just getting started. Tonight I will eat my fill.

Pulling Bianca into my arms, I crush her lips under mine. She melts in my embrace and presses her body close. I push my tongue inside her mouth—she tastes like coffee and cherry Danish. She moans and snakes her tongue along mine, then pulls away, breathing hard. She groans, a guttural, desperate sound, and charges back into the fray.

Our kiss is like a sparring match between two rivals, fighting for domination. Only we're not rivals. Our end goal is the same—sex and love and falling asleep in each other's arms. Waking up tomorrow and doing it all over again.

Sharing an unbreakable bond.

I end the kiss. "Bend over the desk."

She sucks my bottom lip between her teeth, nipping me sharply before obeying. I take a moment to enjoy the sight of her smooth back, her curtain of long, dark hair and the way it frames her pale skin. Her luscious arse pushes towards me, her juices coating her inner thighs. I lay my hands on her skin and savour the feel of her softness, and then I take my cock in hand and slowly feed it inside her gloriously tight cunt.

The moment I enter her, our bond begins to form. She groans as I push deeper, a dark, primal noise, and I know she feels it, too: a total and overwhelming sense of belonging to one another.

The bond heightens our senses, our responses to each

other. She meets me thrust for thrust, pushing back as I ram forward, perfect synchronicity, sinking so deep inside her my cock is buried to the hilt.

She cries out. "More. I want more."

My tail rubs her clit. Her back arches, lifting her off the desk. She supports her weight on her arms and looks over her shoulder at me. The heat banked in her eyes is scorching.

Pulling out, I flip her over, perch her on the edge of my desk and slide back inside her tight embrace. She pulls her knees up, and I sink in deeper. I hook my forearms under her legs, and she wraps her arms around my neck.

Our eyes meet, and I can't look away.

She is beauty and wit and passion.

My beloved.

The pressure builds inside me again, and I know it won't be long until I come. Tugging me down to meet her lips, our kiss is more desperate than our need to breathe. Her body tightens, stiffens. She jerks against me as her orgasm washes over her, breaking our kiss to scream obscenities at the ceiling.

I can't hold out much longer. She's caught me in the vice-like grip of her cunt as she comes and comes and comes. I fuck her like my life depends on it, harder, faster, and only when I feel her body begin to relax, do I finally let go, my own orgasm more intense for the waiting. I cry her name and hold her close. My body shatters apart and reforms, only to shatter again.

I am spent.

Our breath mingles in the aftermath of our passion. My knees feel weak and it's an effort to stand. I stumble back and fall into a chair, and Bianca slips from the desk and crawls into my lap, sweaty, sticky and satiated.

"Your skin feels cooler," she mutters against my neck.

"Think of my body like a furnace, and lust as the fuel," I tell her, closing my eyes as sleep tugs at me. "The hotter the fuel burns, the more pressure in the furnace."

"But if you let some of that heat out...."

"The furnace cools down," I confirm with a smile. I knew she'd get it, my clever little human.

Nestling her head against my neck, her hair tickles my chest. "I guess that means I'll have to monitor your heat valve more closely from now on. Make sure you don't overheat again."

I open one eye and stare down at her. "Is *heat valve* a euphemism for my dick?"

"Maybe." She grins at me. "Yes."

I grin back. "Then yes, I suggest you check it at least twice a day. Preferably more."

Bianca laughs, her soft body shaking against mine, then she pouts and makes a disappointed sound as I force my human façade back into place and prepare for sleep to overtake me.

Finally.

But then Bianca kisses my cheek, stands and gathers her clothing and I panic. I grab her hand and tug, tumble her back into my lap. "And where do you think you're going?"

Pushing a lock of sweat-soaked hair off her face, she says, "Someone has to run this joint." At my frown, she adds, "I'm just going to do the rounds, and then I'll be back."

Now it's my turn to pout. "Promise?" I finally have my woman in my arms and every cell of my being is screaming at me to hold her tight and drink her in, to pleasure her, worship her, as is her due.

I needn't have worried.

Bianca laughs and then lays the slowest, hottest kiss of my life on my mouth. "I promise." She dresses quickly and fixes her hair, pausing before she unlocks the door. "Oh, and, Rugaal, if you're not asleep by the time I get back, I'm going to fuck you into a coma."

My cock twitches at the hint of challenge. "Yes, beloved." And when she leaves the room, I know in my heart that not once in all my two hundred–plus years of living have I ever fought so hard to stay awake.

I SAW

I CONQUERED

I CAME

For my pseudo-sister, Amy.
You're really stuck with me now!
Sucker.

I Saw, I Conquered, I Came

Working late at the office, my fat arse. And apparently it was my fat arse that made my boyfriend think he had every right to cheat on me.

Because fat chicks aren't human, didn't ya know?

We don't have feelings, or if we do, they're so buried under layer upon layer of fat that we're naturally insulated from the realities of dating a cheating arsehole.

My teeth gnash together as tonight's revelations replay in my head. The excuses, the pathetic justifications of his actions that bordered on the ridiculous. The insults he threw at me as I called him on his bullshit.

Stupid, fat bitch.

Yep. That's me. Stupid for expecting I'd ever be anything but his dirty little secret, and unapologetically fat, which obviously makes me a complete bitch.

So here I am, alone again, at ten minutes before closing on a Friday night, standing in front of the ice-cream cabinet in my local deli trying to decide between Chubby Hubby, Coffee Toffee Crunch, and Chocolate Fudge Brownie.

Chocolate Fudge Brownie wins, mostly because *hello*, brownies, but also because it's the last one standing. A stalwart of chocolaty goodness all alone amidst a sea of salted peanut butter caramels and boysenberry swirls.

Rich and sweet and chunky and completely out of place.

Like me.

I reach in to grab that sad-looking pint at the same time as the man standing beside me. His hand brushes mine as he makes a play for the ice-cream, the warmth of his skin shocking to my senses in the cool, refrigerated air, but I'm quicker. My fingers wrap around the container, yank it free from its isolation and drop it into my shopping basket.

Felicity: one.

Random Stranger: nil.

It's a small victory, and possibly a petty one, but one I desperately need right now.

Avoiding eye contact yet flashing a mildly apologetic smile at my hapless rival, I move to squeeze past him down the narrow aisle. He doesn't budge, so I try a more demure approach and drop my gaze from his chest to the floor.

"Excuse me," I mutter softly.

But instead of stepping aside and avoiding confrontation, as most people would, he crosses his arms over his chest and continues to stand there, blocking my escape route.

What is this guy's problem?

Taking a deep breath to cool my resurging anger, I lift my chin, a stern lecture about his lack of manners on the tip of my tongue, but the moment my gaze meets his... *holy fuck!*

Using my tongue to scold him is the last thing I should be using it for.

Even with a scowl plastered across his brow, the man could stop traffic. Looking like he just rolled out of bed with his sandy-coloured hair all sexy and mussed, and the hint of a five o'clock shadow dusting a chiselled jaw, his startling blue eyes freeze me in place with their directness, yet burn me with their intensity.

My girly parts pulse with awareness and my panties grow wet. Pressing my thighs together, I resist the urge to squirm and—wait, is my mouth hanging open?

Oh dear Lord, it is.

Snapping it shut, I swallow hard and suppress a whimper of desire. At least I hope I did. At this distance, he's bound to hear every little sound I make, and the last thing I need is to appear foolish in front of yet another man.

I've already hit my daily quota in that particular department.

Pretending to be more confident than I feel, I pull my shoulders back and attempt to school my features. "Can I help you?"

"You have my ice-cream."

Deep and melodic, his voice slides over me like a warm caress and my insides quiver with arousal. *Oh great.* But he's obviously a crazy person if he thinks I'm handing over my ice-cream without a fight.

"*Your* ice-cream, huh?" I cock one brow. "So which one are you, Ben or Jerry?"

Wait, what? Am I fighting or flirting?

My voice has dropped and taken on a slightly sultry tone, my senses are heightened, my pulse racing—yep, I'm flirting. I just broke up with someone and I'm already flirting with someone else. Whoa! Does that make me a slut? Wait, did I just slut-shame myself? Fuck it. I'm obviously not killing myself over the douchecanoe formerly known as my boyfriend. Anyway, what's that old saying about getting back on the horse?

My combatant looks confused. "I beg your pardon?"

Here goes nothing. "Well the only other name on here is Chocolate Fudge Brownie, and you don't really look like a Chocolate Fudge Brownie, so...."

Mirroring my expression, he cocks one perfect eyebrow. "What do I look like, then, in your *expert* opinion?"

"Expert?" I scoff. "Oh right, because all fat chicks are ice-cream experts." *So much for flirting.* Still, I tilt my head and consider him for a moment, letting my gaze drift from his stupidly handsome face, over his ink-blue suit and white shirt and down his long legs all the way to his tanned leather shoes. "Hmm... you strike me as more of a Chubby Hubby."

His eyes widen and his brows shoot up to his hairline. "Chubby Hubby?"

Pretending to be shocked, I cue the sarcasm. "Oh, you're not a fan of chubby? What a surprise."

"Actually"—in a lightning fast move he comes at me, forcing me back against the freezer door—"I have a great deal of respect for chubby. But I want what I want. And what I want is Chocolate Fudge Brownie."

The door at my back is icy cold and makes me shiver, the sudden chill causes my nipples to harden and stretch the thin fabric of my little black dress. The slinky little number leaves nothing to the imagination, clinging to every curve God gave me and then some. I'd worn it especially for my boyfriend and paired it with my favourite hot-pink stilettos.

Staring at myself in the mirror, I'd felt sexy, confident, powerful. Seeing my reflection in the mirrored doors of the elevators as I'd walked away from him and the swizzle-stick he'd been banging behind my back was less empowering, even if I did walk away with my head held high. My confidence was dented, my power turned to anger, and sexy?

Yeah right.

But as those elevator doors slid shut and I watched the lights counting down my journey to the lobby, as my hands curled into fists at my sides and the urge to ram my stiletto heels through the douchecanoe's balls screamed inside my head, I had a moment of complete clarity.

Fuck 'em!

I deserve better.

Now I'm standing in front of this stranger, growing hotter by the second as his gaze slowly drifts down my body and all the way back up again, lingering on my cleavage and my frosty nipples. The air around us stills and the rest of the world drops away. All I hear is the sound of our breathing and the quiet hum of the fridges at my back. He leans a little closer, tilts his head and I think... I think he's going to... kiss me?

Score!

Until I feel my shopping basket move. And I know I didn't move it.

Straightening to my meagre height, I yank the basket away from my opponent and feel the ice-cream tub drop back inside. "Oh my God."

"Yes?" He grins at me, and my knees threaten to give out.

What the hell is wrong with me tonight?

I laugh in disbelief, although if I'm being honest, a guy using me for his own gain isn't really all that unbelievable. "Were you seriously trying to seduce me so you could steal *my* ice-cream?"

"*Your* ice-cream?" He laughs. "You haven't paid for it yet, sweetheart."

My eyes narrow and it takes all my restraint not to jab my finger into his solid-looking chest. "Call me sweetheart again. I dare you."

He leans closer, invading my personal space with his body and his heat and his cologne that smells like how I imagine sex would smell on a deserted tropical island—sea spray and citrus and sun-drenched sand. His mouth hovers by my ear and his warm breath caresses my neck. "Sweet. Heart."

Forget wet. My panties are soaked. Five minutes with this guy, in a deli, fighting over ice-cream, and I'm ready to climb him like a fucking tree.

Still....

"You do know they make this flavour in frozen yoghurt too, right?"

"Frozen yoghurt?" He pulls away, his grin twisting with disgust. "Lady, I've had one shit of a day and fro-yo just isn't going to cut it." His stare is intense, all playfulness gone from his expression, and to my surprise, I'm disappointed by the loss of his smile. "I want the real deal." He points at the pint. "I want that ice-cream."

His arrogance turns my disappointment to anger and my grip tightens on the basket. *Stupid, fat bitch.* "Yeah, well, I want a boyfriend who doesn't fuck skinny bimbos behind my back, so I guess we're both shit out of luck."

Annnd... it's official.

I suck at flirting.

His eyes widen and he seems taken aback by my words, as though he doesn't quite know what to do with this information I've just spewed all over him. And then his eyes narrow and he searches my face, curiosity bending his brow. "Your boyfriend cheated on you?" He almost sounds concerned.

If it wasn't for the fact that he'd just tried to steal my ice-cream, I'd almost believe him. "Yes, he did. With Amanda from accounting, whom I can now confirm, despite popular opinion, is a natural blonde."

I'm not joking either—copping an eyeful of bimbo bush was just one of tonight's many and varied humiliations—but when he starts to laugh, the sound is so infectious that I start laughing too. The silliness of the situation I've found myself in washes away any final remnants of regret or sadness or anger at seeing my boyfriend balls deep in another woman on the floor of his office.

But I'm caught off guard when bubbling up from underneath all that emotion is the great sucking wound of loneliness. And it hurts.

So. Fucking. Much.

My laughter fades, then dies. And so does my appetite. "Here. You take it." I shove the basket at him. "I'm not hungry anymore."

Over the loudspeaker, the cashier announces that the store is closing.

Time to go.

As I leave the deli and exit into the frigid winter night, I regret leaving my coat behind in the douchecanoe's office. In my defence, I was in shock when I dropped it. I could have gone back for it, I guess, but nah, fuck that.

I mean, what's the cost of a new coat compared to standing tall as you walk away from an arsehole without looking back?

If only wrapping myself in dignity stopped me from freezing my tits off.

"Hey, sweetheart! Wait up."

What the...?

"Chubby Hubby? What do you want?"

He hands me an ice-cream-laden eco-friendly shopping bag. "Here. You forgot this." And then he takes off his jacket and drapes it around my shoulders, drops his gaze to the ice bullets expanding my bra again and smirks.

"What are you doing?"

I try not to moan as the warmth from his jacket soaks into my chilled flesh, and a mixture of that dreamy cologne and what I can only assume is his natural male musk permeates my senses. Am I drooling? I think I'm drooling, but my face is so cold I can't tell.

"You looked chilly," he says as he pulls the jacket closed over my chest, gently brushing his knuckles over my nipples in the process. *Hello!* "And my name is Jason, by the way."

I suck in a breath at his closeness and get another lungful of his delicious scent. "Felicity. My name is Felicity." And there goes my voice again, sounding all sultry and shit. Why does it keep doing that? Haven't we already established I suck at flirting?

"It's nice to meet you, Felicity." He holds out his hand, and I take it in mine. His grip is firm, his palm warm. He's slow to let go. "And I'm sorry I acted like a dick in there. It has been a *really* bad day, but that's no excuse for my behaviour."

My mouth falls open again. I've never had a guy apologise to me before. Ever. Unsure what else to do, I shrug. Unsure what else to say, I ask him, "So why was your day bad?"

He shoves his hands in his pockets, shuffles his feet and avoids my gaze. "For pretty much the same reason as you."

"You caught your boyfriend cheating on you?"

His mouth twists. "I caught my girlfriend cheating on me. I went home for lunch and found her on the couch with our neighbour."

"How do you know they weren't just talking?"

He shoots me a look that smacks of betrayal and his voice is hard, tinged with hurt. "Let's see now. I think his dick in her mouth was my first clue."

Well, I feel stupid. "Oh."

We stand there, staring at each other as awkward silence fills the air between us like a bubble. A bubble he bursts when he blurts out, "Can I walk you home?"

I smile. "Sure. Better than standing out here on the pavement freezing to death." The silence is only slightly less awkward as we walk the five paces to the steps leading up to my front door. "Thanks." His confusion is amusing, his gaze shifting from me to the door and back again. I take pity on him; he did walk me home, after all. "I live in the apartment above the deli."

A lopsided smile stretches across his face. "Ah. I thought maybe you were trying to blow me off."

Juggling the shopping bag with my purse, I search for my keys. Keys found, I unlock the door and push it open, then turn to face Jason, now shivering as he stands on the bottom step, his hands still shoved in his pockets in a futile attempt to ward off the chilly night air. "Thank you for this." I hold up the shopping bag. "You didn't have to."

He flashes that sexy grin again. "I know."

Curiosity getting the better of me, I tilt my head to one side and frown as my gaze drifts over him, my would-be knight in shining armour. "Why are you being nice to me?"

"Can't a guy be nice to a girl without having an agenda?"

"Not in my experience, no."

"Sweetheart, you've been hanging out with the wrong type of men."

"I can't argue with that." The chilled air whips around me, and I mourn the loss of his warmth and his scent as I slide his jacket off my shoulders and hand it back to him. "Thank you for walking me home, Jason."

"Anytime," he says and backs away from the steps. "I guess this is goodnight, then?"

Of course it is. But what did I expect, a marriage proposal? Maybe not, but a *"Hey, would you like to hang out and see what happens?"* would have been nice, too. "Yeah, I guess so."

My gut twists with disappointment.

But as I watch him walk away—very slowly walk away —I think, *Why the fuck am I waiting for him to ask me?* I'm a grown-arse woman with wants and desires all my own and I should be asking him.

My soaked panties agree.

Just as I'm about to call out to him, however, the more cautious side of my brain clamps a hand over my mouth and forces me to see reason. I just met this man, and sure he's wickedly sexy, but how many police reports have started with "Well, you see officer, I met this cute guy...."

On the other side of the argument, my rational thinking is pointing out the fact that he could have just taken the ice-cream and run, but he didn't. He gave it to me, and he gave me his jacket to wear even though it's freezing out, and offered to walk me home even though he had no idea where I live or how long he'd have to suffer the cold before we got there. And while it's entirely possible that it was all a manipulation to get his hands on my ice-cream, it was also kinda sweet, and I could really use some sweet right now.

And I don't just mean the ice-cream.

Besides, Jason might be a head taller than me and rocking what appeared to be a killer six-pack under that slim-fit business shirt, but I definitely have the weight advantage. If he does turn out to be a psycho serial killer, I reckon I could take him.

Still, I'm nervous. Inviting strange men into my home less than twenty minutes after meeting them is not my usual gig. In fact it's pretty much the opposite of what I would usually do.

An icy wind swirls around me, makes me shiver, and I see Jason wrap his arms around his middle as the wind pulls at his jacket. Maybe it's time to warm us both up a bit. Maybe, *definitely*, it's time to step out of my comfort zone.

Voice raised against the wind, I call out, "Hey, Jason?"

He turns around. "Yeah?"

"Would you like to come inside and, I don't know... talk?"

He walks back to the bottom of the steps and pins me with that intense stare again. "Not really." But he takes a step closer.

Okay. "Would you like to come inside, watch a movie and eat ice-cream?"

He takes two more steps. "Warmer...."

Biting back a smile, I finally ask, "Would you like to come inside, watch a movie, eat ice-cream and..." I feel my face flush with heat, "fuck?"

He stops on the step below me, his face now level with mine. He slides his hand under my dress and trails his fingertips up my inner thigh, stopping just below my pussy and drawing lazy little circles on my flesh. His voice is soft, dark. "I thought you'd never ask."

Oh. Dear. Lord.

Did I say soaked? Because I think my panties just drowned and went to pantie heaven. I swallow hard and lean towards him, his mouth, that wicked grin, so close, so tempting... but I pull away before our lips meet and turn towards the door.

I'm horny, not easy.

Jason snaps his teeth together. "Tease." Then he follows me inside and up the stairs to my apartment.

Taking his jacket, I hang it on a hook by the door, and then fish the ice-cream out of the shopping bag and grab two spoons from the kitchen. "So, what do you want to do first? Movie, ice-cream or...."

"Fuck," he says as he takes the ice-cream from my hands and sets it down on the kitchen table. "Definitely fuck."

The spoons clatter to the floor as his mouth crashes against mine and he swallows my moan of approval. His hands glide down my body, and I can feel him through my dress, hot and searching, eager and ready.

Just like me.

"Your bed. Where's your bed?" he says, nuzzling my throat and nibbling my earlobe.

"No. No bed." I push him back, making sure he can see me, hear me. Understand me. "I want you. Here. Now. Lights on. Pants off. I want you to give me what I always want and never get—hard, dirty, no-holds-barred fucking."

He sucks in a breath, his nostrils flare and his eyes darken. "That is the hottest damn thing any woman has ever said to me."

My fingers shake as I reach down and grab the hemline of my dress, slowly dragging the clingy, black sheath up and off my body, revealing my pale, wobbly flesh and the black lacy bra and panties trying in vain to hold it all in.

His eyes grow wide, and I can't tell if it's with lust or fear. Until he pushes me against the refrigerator, lifts my legs around his hips, and shoves his tongue down my throat.

Lust. Definitely lust.

"If you want dirty, I'll give you dirty," he says, breaking the kiss to nibble along my jaw. "But you have to give me something in return."

I try to ignore the fridge magnet digging into my back even as I'm loving his fingers digging into my thighs. "What do you want?"

Please don't say ice-cream.

Please don't say ice-cream.

Please don't say ice-cream.

"Your shoes."

My... *what?*

He wants my hot-pink snakeskin, five-inch stiletto, bargain-basement knock-offs? Brow scrunched in confusion, I ask the only question I can think of in such an unfamiliar situation. "Huh?"

A rumbling chuckle shakes him and he presses forward again, kissing me until my toes curl. "You could have walked around naked with the words 'follow me home and fuck me' spray-painted across your tits and it would have been more subtle than those goddamn shoes. I don't care what we do tonight, but those sexy stripper heels do not come off. Deal?"

Excitement fires low in my belly and I nod. "Deal."

Jason carries me to the kitchen table and plants my arse down beside the pint of ice-cream. His fingers are warm against my skin as he spreads my knees apart, his tented trousers brushing the inside of my thighs as he stands between them.

Leaning back on my hands, I let my gaze slide over him, watching him unbutton his shirt in what can only be described as the most torturously slow striptease in history. I want to rip that shirt apart and watch the buttons fly across the room, but as each button popped reveals a hint of more tight, tanned muscle, I console myself with the knowledge that, for tonight at least, this man is *all mine*.

The last button pops and I sit forward again, slide my hands under his business shirt and push it off his broad shoulders. The soft white cotton slides down his arms and falls to the floor with a quiet swoosh, and he stands there staring down at me, his grin gone, his eyes dark, his chest rising and falling under my fingertips.

Swallowing down my nervousness, and pretending I know *waaay* more about seducing a man like Jason than I actually do, I slowly drag my fingers over his chest and explore every buff inch on the way down. His hands are on my thighs, stroking, squeezing, creeping closer towards my pussy.

My hands are at his belt, the metallic buckle cold against my fingers as I pull the leather free, but as I reach for the button at his waist I freeze, a cold trickle of reality running down my spine and shocking me out of my lustful fantasy.

I snap my gaze to Jason's, my eyes wide, my heart sinking fast.

"What's wrong?"

I want to cry. "I don't have any condoms. Shit." I can't believe my evening is about to be ruined. Again.

I want sex, dammit, with the sexy hunk of a man standing between my spread thighs and I want it now. Maybe I could run down to the deli—except they're shut. *Fuck*. No, not fuck. No fucking tonight, folks.

Fuuuck....

"I don't normally carry one around either," Jason says, reaching into his back pocket. "So I hope you don't mind, but I took the liberty of buying a pack. Just in case." An unmistakable flood of gratitude and relief flows through me and I kiss the ever-loving life out of him. I also tear his fly open and slide my hand inside his boxer-briefs, wrapping my fingers around his rather impressive cock. He gasps. "I guess you're okay with it."

Smiling sheepishly, I take the box of condoms from him, pop it open and take one out. "A six-pack, huh?"

He grins as he toes off his shoes, then shucks his trousers and underwear. "Call me optimistic."

"I think I'd rather call it a challenge." My smile widens. "And ribbed for my pleasure, I see."

Jason winks. "I'm nothing if not a giver."

I rip the foil open with my teeth and toss the packet over my shoulder. "Come here." Taking his cock in my hand, I enjoy his sudden intake of breath, the way his stomach quivers and his muscles tense as I slowly roll the condom over the full length of him.

The long, hard, thick length of him.

I bite my lip as anticipation flares inside me.

Jason's fingers tangle in the lace of my panties and he yanks me forward so my butt rests precariously on the edge of the table. Placing his big hand in the middle of my chest, he gently pushes me down until I'm flat on my back. Grabbing a chair, he seats himself between my legs. When I raise a brow, he says, "What? I always eat at the table."

"E-eat?" I swallow hard but my eyes shoot wide open. *Is he about to do what I think he's about to do?* Just to be sure, I say, half-jokingly, "Please tell me you're not talking about the ice-cream."

His mouth kicks up in that wicked grin of his. "Now there's an interesting idea. Can't say I've ever licked ice-cream off a girl's pussy before, but I did promise you dirty." And he reaches for the pint that's slowly melting on the table.

"No!"

His hand stops a mere inch from its target. "What, you don't like the ice-cream idea?" He frowns at me as I stare at him, my mouth flapping open and shut like a fish out of water, silent, stunned. "Or is it me eating your pussy that's freaking you out? What's the matter? Don't you like oral sex?"

"No. I mean yes. I mean...." How do I explain this to him? My cheeks heat and I turn my head to hide my embarrassment, to hide my ignorance, but the words come out anyway. "I don't know if I like it or not. I've never had a guy go down on me before."

"Why the fuck not?"

Jason sounds genuinely baffled, which makes me feel even more embarrassed. I move to sit up, to close my legs, to feel less open, less vulnerable, but he doesn't let me. He's on his feet again and leaning over me, pressing his body between my thighs and pinning my hands to the table.

"Look at me, Felicity."

I turn my head to face him and look up at his curious expression, but it's hard to focus on anything with his cock jutting up between my legs, pressing against my mound, pushing the lace of my panties against my clit in the most *ah-may-zing* way. I can't help the moan that escapes me, nor can I help but notice the way he starts rocking his hips, gently smooshing that lace into my clit over and over again as he speaks to me.

"Is it because you're curvy?"

Eyes rolling back in my head, I say, "You can say the F-word, Jason." He rocks against me again, and my hips roll up to meet him. His eyes close and he groans. I lick my suddenly dry lips. "It's all right. I am what I am, and what I

44

am is fat. And yes, my size was the most common excuse given."

Jason grunts, a sound of disgust. "Fucking amateurs. And I bet every single one of them expected you to suck their cocks, didn't they?"

I nod, embarrassed again, imagining what he must think of me now.

But his expression softens, his mouth twitching into a lopsided grin. "Well then, it's a good thing for you I'm no amateur."

I snort a laugh. "As if I'd know the difference."

He winks. "Trust me, you'll know." Letting go of my wrists, he trails his fingers down my body, hooks them into the waist of my panties and drags them down my legs until they dangle from my foot, snagged on the stiletto I'm not allowed to remove.

His fingers glide across my mound, and I send up a silent prayer, thankful I remembered to wax. Then he shoots me another one of those panty-melting grins, and says, "Buckle your seat belt, sweetheart."

My body shakes with laughter. But when I feel his tongue lash against my clit I almost jump out of my skin. Holy shit that feels great. And then he does it again. And again, and again and again, until I think I'm going crazy.

My back arches off the table and my hands grab at nothing, clenching around thin air and then springing open again, reaching for something, anything to anchor me to this point in time and hold me here for as long as fucking possible.

I'm pretty sure my mouth is hanging open. And I don't care. For the first time in my life, a man is going down on me and I intend to enjoy every damn second of it.

I moan his name as I feel his fingers slide inside me, but then—

"Fuck that's cold!"

He laughs out loud and his shoulders jiggle my thighs where he holds them wide. I lift my head and see him watching me over my stomach, a wide grin stretched across his face as he pushes the pint of ice-cream against my clit.

The cardboard container is ice cold and the shock of it heightens my awareness of him, makes me more responsive to his heat as he laves my pussy with the broad side of his tongue.

My breathing hitches and I'm hot all over. My back arches again and I can't keep still. I reach down and feel for him, run my fingers through his hair and tug him closer as I buck my hips against his mouth.

He sucks and licks my clit, hard little flicks of his tongue followed by urgent open-mouthed kisses that make me melt. His fingers piston in and out, hitting me deep and with bruising intensity and then I'm coming. I'm coming hard, and it is so much better than I ever thought it would be.

My body shakes and my brain melts, my hips thrust and my toes curl. I'm falling, I'm writhing, I'm praying to God that it never ends, that the man with his head between my legs never stops—

And then I'm sucking in breath after breath, satiated beyond belief.

But Jason's not done with me yet. As he stands, he wipes his mouth with the back of his hand and stares down at me, his intense blue gaze devouring every inch of my soft body. Grabbing my legs, he lifts them up and holds them to his chest so my feet—and my sexy stripper heels—stick up on either side of his head, and then he turns to press a kiss on my ankle. "Now we fuck."

I've barely caught my breath, but his cock is pushing for entry. I bite my lip and moan as he stretches me open and fills me up. And oh my Lord, when he starts to move, sliding in and pulling out, slowly at first, *sooo* slowly, I feel every inch he's giving me and know without a doubt that yes, that ribbed condom is 100 percent completely and totally for my pleasure.

Holy fuck.

His hands are hot as he holds my ankles and spreads my legs apart. If I lift my head, I can see his cock gliding in and out and in and out of me, slick and shining with my own arousal, and it makes me feel so open, so dirty. *So sexy.* And the way he's looking at me, like he wants to eat me out all over again....

Oh my fucking God, yes please!

"What are you thinking about, sweetheart?"

What am I thinking about? During the best sex I've ever had in my boring little life? "Besides, thank God we both love Chocolate Fudge Brownie?"

"Well it is the best ice-cream ever," he says, grinning again. "But that's not really the answer I was looking for."

I flash him a grin of my own. "I was thinking about doing something like this."

I may not be as experienced as I would like, but I'm no novice either. Tugging my legs free of his hold, I cross them across his chest and rest my ankles on his strong shoulders. If I thought I felt full before, it's nothing compared to how I feel now that everything has tightened two-fold.

Jason's head falls back and he groans, guttural, almost animalistic. "Oh yeah. I like the way you think."

His fingers dig into my thighs, bruising my soft skin as he thrusts faster, harder, hitting me deeper and making me cry out again as another orgasm tears through my body and makes me undulate with pleasure.

Pinning his wild stare with my own, I demand, "More."

"Play with yourself." The steel in his voice says it's not a request.

Letting go of the table edge, I slide one hand between my legs and the other to my breast. My nipple is hard but not from the cold. I slip my hand inside the lacy cup of my bra and tug at my sensitive flesh, feel the weight of my breast dragging down as I pull up, and enjoy the slight pain that adds to my pleasure.

Between my legs is warm and wet. My clit is still sensitive from Jason's tongue lashing and lace smashing, and it makes me jump when I touch it. If I reach down just a little farther, I can feel the rubber-covered steel of his cock as he fucks me. I push down a little, applying pressure as he glides in and out.

His mouth falls open on a moan. "Oh fuck, do that again."

I do it again and again and again, tease and torture and pleasure him the way he's been doing to me.

Jason stares down at me, watches me, never breaking eye-contact. "You're so fucking gorgeous," he growls, right before his fingers tighten on my thighs and he pumps his hips against me, slams his cock inside me fast and hard like a demented madman. Roars at the ceiling like the beast he is as he shoots his load.

And I'm right there with him, screaming his name as I chase my own release.

Moments later, the only sound filling the air around us is that of heavy breathing, and then Jason pulls out and slumps down into the chair. The loss of his hot skin and hard muscle chills my flesh, but that's not the only thing making me shiver.

Sitting up, I hug my arms around my waist, not just for warmth but to hide my belly, too. Now that the heat of lust has cooled, I'm feeling vulnerable again. I just fucked a complete stranger on my kitchen table.

What was I thinking?

But Jason's too busy disposing of the condom to pay any attention to my insecurities, and when he returns to the table he cups my face in his strong hands and lifts my mouth to his.

"Thank you." His words whisper over my lips before he pushes forwards and slips his tongue inside my mouth and makes my toes curl for a whole other reason.

Good Lord the man can kiss.

Heat flares to life inside me and suddenly my arms are wrapped around *his* middle instead of my own and I drink him in, his flavour, his scent, that rich male musk and a hint of cologne mixed with the smell of sweat and sex. When he pulls back, he's smiling. Not cocky, not grinning, but smiling.

Warm and genuine and sexy as hell.

Annnd my bra has magically come undone.

Eyes narrowed as Jason strips me of the last of my clothing, I say, "Dare I ask what you're thinking about?"

He licks his lips. "I'm thinking I'd like some ice-cream now."

I pick up the pint and take off the lid. Condensation runs over my fingers and the ice-cream inside has melted. It's squishy but not a total write-off. I pick out a brownie chunk and eat it, find another and feed it to him, laugh as he nibbles my fingers. "We need spoons."

His grin is back. "I have a much better idea." Relieving

me of the pint, Jason squashes it in his fist so cool, mushy ice-cream spills out of the tub and all over my naked breasts.

I squeal with delight as my lover's head descends, as he pushes me back on the table and crawls on up here with me. His tongue is warm and tickles my flesh as he licks and sucks the sticky, gooey mess from my skin.

When he reaches for another condom, I watch him sheath that impressive beast once more, and as he slides inside my pussy and bends his head to suck ice-cream off my breast, one thought—one perfect, sexy, dirty thought—pops inside my head.

"Best. Ice-cream. Ever."

PUSHING ROPE

For my writing tribe, for keeping me sane...ish...

Pushing Rope

S ucking on my cigarillo and staring into space, my valet's voice is a nagging tickle inside my eardrums. And as much as I would like to drown him out—or simply drown him—I cannot.

"...you even listening to me?"

"What?"

Jonathon slowly rolls his shoulders, the irritation sluicing off him in waves. He's fun to annoy. "I said, would you like me to refresh your bath? The water has gone cold."

Shifting my gaze to the surface of the water, I watch my flaccid cock as it bobs around between my legs like a neglected bath toy, and then I heave a sigh and nod at the stool beside the tub. "The only thing that needs refreshing is my brandy glass."

Cigarillo clamped between my teeth, I brace my hands on either side of the bath and haul my arse out of the tub. Water runs down my body in cool rivulets that track over the rigid muscles of my chest and stomach. As it trickles down my thighs and drips off the end of my useless knob, I remember how much I used to loathe the stuff.

Water, such a contradictory substance. Able to give life as easily as it takes it, it is sickeningly pure and yet terrifyingly dark. It's also my father's weapon of choice. Want to cleanse the weak of evil? Water. Want to dedicate your soul to a higher purpose? Water. Need to wipe out the whole of human existence except your BFF and his menagerie? Water.

I feared and hated the stuff.

Until I met Nadia, my lovely little naiad.

Not that I'd known what she was when I met her—half-dead, stuck at the bottom of an empty well and reeking of filth. I only found her because I'd stopped to take a piss and freaked out when I saw her haunted expression leering up at me like a spectre from my past.

Unsure of her origins, I was tempted to leave her down there, but there was something about her, something that called to me, so I fished her out. When she begged me for water, I was tempted to drop her back down the hole she came from, but then that feeling, that *something* urged me on. I scooped her up, putrescence and all, then carried her to the edge of the nearest stream and tossed her in. I figured if she drowned, so be it, at least she'd have her precious water, but I'd be fucked if I was getting any closer to it than I had to.

What happened next was... *unexpected*.

The little ragamuffin I'd pitched into the stream came up looking more like a fucking angel than the horror movie reject I'd pulled out of the ground, the water restoring her lost vitality until she'd practically glowed with life.

She had a slim yet soft body that dipped and swelled in all the right places, creamy skin and long honey-brown hair that reached down below the gentle curve of her arse. Her small, firm breasts were tipped with the most delicate rosy nipples I'd ever seen, but it was her eyes that caught and held my attention. Eyes of such a pure, crystalline blue they reminded me of Heaven. And that *something* I'd felt earlier suddenly had a name.

Home.

As I watched her splash about in the stream, I was entranced by her beauty, ensnared by her aura of sensuality. Before I knew what I was doing, I stood hip deep in water with a goddess in my arms, her tongue down my throat and my cock so engorged it still amazes me I didn't pass out from the lack of blood to my brain.

Nadia was so grateful for my assistance, she fucked me stupid for three days straight.

And water got crossed off the list of things that scare the shit out of me.

Fast-forward a few centuries and she's still my go-to booty call. It's the eyes. I get lost in the fathomless depths of her eyes, get a glimpse of my old life before I followed my brother Lucifer and took a swan dive into damnation. Before I became... *this*.

Yeah, yeah, I know. I'm Asmodeus, a prince of Hell, the archdemon of lust, a paragon of lasciviousness and desire. I am *literally* sex on legs.

What's so bad about being me, right?

Well, there's the truth curse Lucifer saddled me with so I could never lie to him, then there's the bum leg that requires the use of a walking cane because hey, that fall from grace was a fucking long way down and didn't come with airbags.

And, oh yeah, I can't get an erection to save my life, so... there's that.

Asmodeus, the prince of lust, has erectile dysfunction.

Now there's a headline for you.

Suffice to say it's problematic. Without sex to curb my lust for flesh, my desires will turn dark, will become less carnal, more carnivorous. And personally I'd rather eat a woman out, not, you know, *eat* her.

And who do I have to thank for this little predicament?

Nadia.

My little water witch has done something to me, but I'm fucked if I know what. Or why. But I know it's her. Naiads are notoriously jealous creatures.

The last time I saw her, I spent a whole week seeing to her every whim, fulfilling her every wish. Fucking her every which way she wanted, and what she wanted... *fuuuck*. Let's just say it's a rare woman who can teach *me* new tricks in the bedroom.

On any other day, just the thought of Nadia and her wicked sexual appetites would have my cock springing to attention and my fingers hitting the speed dial, but not now. Not today.

Not for three fucking months.

"Your brandy, my lord."

Swirling the aged amber liquid in the glass, I savour its fragrance. Ordinarily the rich, sweet scent would help calm my busy mind, would ease the onslaught of agitated thoughts marching through my head, but not this time. I throw it down in one swift swallow, then drop my cigar stub inside the glass and listen to it die with a hiss.

The buzz of the alcohol is short-lived and does little to alleviate my irritation. Jonathon's eyes narrow but he says nothing, taking the glass from my outstretched hand with practiced patience.

He returns with a towel and dries my body with an expert touch, then slides a silken robe over me and ties it about my waist. I heave a sigh, neither action piques my interest as it should. When he removes his glasses and stares into my eyes, the corner of my mouth twitches.

I really should stop him, but as his lips graze over mine and his tongue flicks inside my mouth, teasing, tempting, I moan in surrender. Leaning into him, I feel the heat of his body through the thin cotton of his shirt. My hand finds his nape, pulls him tighter against me. I'd forgotten how sweet he tastes, or perhaps that's the brandy.

Angling him back against the bathroom wall, I press the full length of my body against his and deepen our kiss. Like all his incubi brethren, Jonathon is lean and hard. He is strength and sex and wantonness, designed to draw his lovers to him then drive them out of their minds with lust. But I am Asmodeus, the grand poobah of getting it on... when I can get it up. If anyone is to be driven out of their minds tonight, it will not be me.

But Jonathon is determined to try.

His clever fingers slip under my robe and juggle my balls in the most delicious way, and when he licks my throat and nips at my jaw, my pulse races with excitement. My body is humming with pleasure, delighting in the feel of my valet's firm yet gentle caress. My cock should be as hard as granite—but it's not. The stupid, stubborn, godforsaken mockery of my manhood remains limp and lifeless, and I am flooded once more with frustration.

Easing away from Jonathon, I try to mask my disappointment.

He frowns and replaces his glasses. "Perhaps a visit to a human doctor is warranted. Try some of those little blue pills their males are so fond of."

I point to my walking cane. "I don't think so."

"I hear Gluttony has in his possession a foie gras that is particularly fine." When I raise my brow at him, he explains with an undertone of glee. "It's made from the livers of French chefs, fattened on their own signature dishes until their internal organs exploded. Your brother's valet describes it as 'rich and buttery with a just a hint of sweet irony.' Should I make a call?"

Grinding my teeth together, I shake my head. "No, thank you, Jonathon. I'm not *there* yet."

He *tsks* at me as I take my cane and hobble towards the door, then says something for which I would kill a lesser man. "There is one other possibility. Dare I suggest the mighty Asmodeus, patron saint of man-whores everywhere... is in love?"

I turn and shove the point of my cane into the solid wall of his chest. "I am not some lowly incubus who can only get it up for his beloved." Chastened by his hurt expression, I mumble, "No offence, Jonathon."

His hurt turns to pique as he grips the point of my cane and shoves it back at me, almost knocking me on my arse. "As an incubus who will be balls deep in his beloved within the hour, whilst you languish in Limpdicktopia for the foreseeable future, no offence taken, my lord."

My mouth twists into a half-smile. "Touché."

Jonathon drops his gaze and stares at me over the rim of his glasses. "Asmodeus, perhaps Ava and I could join you this evening. Perhaps the company of a female would—"

I hold up my hand to silence him. "I have been in the company of dozens of females since my... *malady* first struck, and while their attentions have been more than pleasurable, not a single one of them made me rise to the occasion, as it were. And as you yourself have witnessed, male attention has fared no better." I yank the door open and step through to my bedroom. "I thank you for your concern, old friend, but I fear there is only one person who can help me now, and the little minx isn't answering her goddamn phone."

"Who's a little minx?"

"Nadia?" Lumbering farther into my room, I spy my lady peeling off her dress.

She finger-waves at me. "Surprise!"

Jonathon coughs discreetly by my side to hide his laughter. "If there'll be nothing else, my lord...?"

I wave him off without another word and zero my focus on the one woman in the world guaranteed to get my dick back on the active duty roster.

And I have its first assignment planned already.

My gaze drifts over my lover, and I drink her in, trying to read her mood, her movements. She's lying on my bed now, belly down and naked—always naked—with her chin propped in her hands and a serene smile aimed squarely at me.

The fall of her hair frames her face like a honey-coloured curtain, highlighting the creaminess of her skin, the rosiness of her lips, the deep, heavenly hue of her eyes. I long to touch her, to soothe the godforsaken ache welling inside me, crush the ancient darkness threatening to consume me, but I'm a stubborn sonofabitch.

I want her to suffer as I have suffered.

She crooks her finger at me, and like a sex-starved simpleton, I am tempted to obey. But if she thinks for an instant she can reel me in as easily as all that, and after what she's done?

I don't think so, lover.

Taking a seat on the well-worn leather couch facing my bed, I grab another cigarillo from the pack, light it up and draw it's sweet taste inside me, and then I blow smoke rings in Nadia's general direction and tap my hand on the vacant seat beside me. Her smile broadens, turns seductive, but her eyes narrow ever so slightly.

"My bedroom, pet. My rules."

A flash of arousal flares in her eyes, colours her cheeks. Blinking slowly, she slips from the bed and stands before me, her proud chin lifting, meeting my challenge. She steps forwards, but I'm not going to make it that easy for her.

For three fucking months she has tormented me from afar, sucked my life force dry. She has no idea how close I came to giving Jonathon the order, telling him to call my brother, Gluttony, and raiding his vile pantry. Without sex I have slowly starved, and it's taking every ounce of what will power remains not to throw her over my knee and spank a confession out of her. But she'll get her comeuppance.

Payback's a bitch.

"Crawl."

The order is spat from my lips, and I watch with satisfaction as her breasts rise and fall with her quick intake of breath. Her tongue flicks over her sumptuous lips, and I watch the movement like a hawk, longing for the time when she'll wrap those soft pink pillows around my blue balls and blow fresh life into my deflated cock.

"Yes, my lord."

Her sweet submission is music to my ears.

Lowering herself to her hands and knees, she moves across the room. It's only a few paces from the bed to the couch, but she's determined to make me wait. As she crawls across the floor ever so slowly, I watch the elegant sway of her body, admire her lovely figure.

The nubile young naiad I pulled from that empty well all those centuries ago is long gone. Her narrow waist has grown a little softer and a lot less narrow, her slender hips have grown plump with a womanly flare they lacked in her youth, and those pert little breasts with the sweet pink nipples have ripened and grown heavy. My mouth waters as I watch them swing back and forth and back and forth as she crosses the room.

I used to think she was the most beautiful thing I'd ever seen.

But now?

There aren't enough words on God's green Earth to describe how perfect my Nadia is.

Her body is so lush, so soft, so fuckable, and as she reaches my feet and stares up at me, I am gripped by an all-encompassing need to pleasure her, to kiss her and hold her and fuck her senseless.

But I can't.

Not until she reverses whatever the fuck she did to me.

And tells me why she did it.

Barely controlling the anger firing through my veins, I take a deep pull on my cigar and lean back on the couch, spreading my arms wide across the top of the cushions. Nadia watches me, her face a picture of caution as she gets to her feet and settles herself on the couch to my right.

As pissed off as I am, I would never hurt her. I promised her a long time ago, after tracking down and slaughtering the arseholes responsible for dropping her down that cesspool of a well, that I would always protect her. Even from me.

Especially from me.

I never wanted my darkness to taint her light.

Tentative fingers reach out and stroke along my thigh, tug the silk of my robe higher to reveal my damaged leg. To all outward appearances I look like any ordinary man, and by *ordinary* I mean I look like every month of a fucking firemen's calendar rolled into one, then sprayed down with an extra dose of awesome.

Except for that fucking leg.

My deformed, knobbly kneed, grotesque leg.

But Nadia doesn't care. Unlike my previous lovers, serious and casual alike, she has never shied away from me. Never treated me as anything less than a whole man, dignified and strong.

Her gentle hand caresses my ruined knee, soothes the phantom aches that plague me still, even after all this time, then she leans down and grazes her soft lips over the puckered flesh of my scars. The unexpected intimacy makes me shiver, and even more surprising, my heart stutters in my chest.

I didn't even know that thing was still switched on.

I drop my hand to stroke her hair and encourage her lips to travel higher, to latch around my cock. Like that was ever going to work. I've never been able to make this woman do anything she didn't want to. Not that she didn't normally enjoy sucking my cock. Normally she couldn't get enough of it, worked it with those sweet, firm lips and that warm, pliant tongue until I was so dazed with lust I couldn't walk, with or without my cane.

Of course, maybe she wasn't interested now it wasn't working properly....

And whose fault was that, hmm?

I scowl. "Nadia?"

She runs the tip of her tongue from my bulbous kneecap to the crease of my leg, making me tremble in delight. "Yes, my lord?" Her voice overflows with sensual promises.

"Aren't you forgetting something?"

She sits back on her haunches and looks up at me, taps

her slender finger against her chin. "Hmm, I don't think so. I'm naked, you're practically naked, my pussy is hot and wet, and your cock is...." She pulls my robe open, but I refuse to look down, choosing instead to keep my gaze fixed on her pretty face.

Brow raised and lips flat, I ask, "My cock is...?"

Her smile dissolves. "Glorious," she says, her voice dripping with awe.

Wait, what?

That wasn't the response I'd expected. Eyes narrowed, I drop my gaze and glare at my deflated dick, only... it's not deflated anymore.

"What the fuck? When did that happen?"

"Hello, handsome." Nadia's fingers are cool, and I suck in a breath as she wraps them around my rock-hard erection. The next thing I know she's swinging herself into my lap, her legs straddling mine and her pussy perfectly positioned to glide along my cock. She rocks her hips and my head falls back. I moan. Loudly.

I'm in Heaven.

The world melts away under her expert touch, my eyes close and my heart soars and— *did my dick just get harder?* Her whimpering would suggest so.

I stub out my cigar.

Nadia slips her hands around my head, roughly grips the short strands of my hair, and drags herself closer. Our lips touch for the first time in three months, and it's as if I'm tasting brandy for the first time in my life. A sudden burst of heat that warms my body from the inside out, a sweetness that tempts, a richness that emboldens. Then my hands are on her, touching her, exploring, probing, grabbing the fleshy globes of her arse and pulling her tighter against my throbbing cock, rubbing her clit with my dick.

Her back arches and a cry escapes her lips. "Mo! By the gods, I love you."

She slams her mouth against mine once more, and our tongues tangle together. I have missed this woman. My woman. *Mine.* Only she's not mine and she never can be. Not truly. I won't allow it. I won't break her heart just to satisfy my own selfish desires.

I won't.

I can't.

Whatever tiny part of me that's still good, still the angel my father wanted me to be, will never allow this precious creature to waste her heart on a monster like me. I will love her body, but I will never lay claim to her heart. She deserves better than that.

Better than me.

A disappointed groan reverberates through my mouth, and Nadia pulls away. "Well that was fun while it lasted."

My head feels light. I look down and watch my cock slowly wilt, watch it list to the side like a sinking ship.

What. The. Fuck?

"Where did my erection go?"

Frustrated and angry, my gaze flicks to the woman in my lap, zeroes in on those big blue eyes of hers. Eyes that watch the world more shrewdly than she ever admits. I sigh darkly and wonder what she sees when she looks at me. I know she's mad at me. I know she's punishing me.

But I still don't know *why.*

"What's going on, pet?"

She glares at me for a moment, then says, "*Sterises tin kardia, sterises to poutso.*"

I recognise her native Greek instantly and mull the words over in my mind. "Deny the heart, deny the cock? What the fuck is that supposed to mean?"

"Exactly what it says on the label, my love. The more you deny your heart's desire, the more your magnificent cock, and in turn you, will suffer."

I stare at her, dumbfounded. "But *why?*"

She cups my face in her gentle hands, staring deep into my eyes and my sorry excuse for a soul. "Because I look at you and I see myself. I see the longing in your eyes, the loneliness in your heart."

I pause for a moment, feeling awkward and raw, hating how easily she sees through me. "What makes you think I have a heart?"

"What makes you think you don't?"

"I'm a demon. A prince of Hell. I'm a Grade-A bastard double-dipped in selfishness and arrogance. Nadia, why would you love *me?* I'm a dick."

Her laughter is warm, her grin sly. "You know girls love a bad boy, especially the bad boy with a heart of gold."

"Ah, now I see where your confusion lies," I say with a weary sigh. "*My* heart is made of lead, my dear. Looks like gold on paper, but it's much more toxic in reality."

Crossing her arms over her chest, she narrows her eyes and frowns at me. "Just say it, you stubborn jackass."

I feign ignorance. "Say what?"

"Okay, if that's how you want to play it, fine. Let me put this to you in terms you'll understand. The curse is a chastity belt. Truth is the key. But hey, if you're content going crazy as you slowly starve to death, be my guest. Or you can grow a pair, admit how you feel about me and get back to the task of filling my deliciously wet pussy with your monster-sized cock." She pauses to toss her hair over her shoulder. "So, are these balls I'm bouncing on just for show, or do you have something to say?"

Oh, I have something to say, all right. "How do you

know it's your curse at work and that I'm not having some sort of... I don't know, mid-life crisis?"

She glares at me. "You're immortal. You don't have a mid-life. And if you *truthfully* didn't love me, the curse wouldn't work."

I stare at her, my eyes wide, my jaw dropped. *Of all the manipulative....* Using my truth curse against me?

Oh, she is clever.

Evil genius clever.

And I fucking adore her for it!

"You little minx!" I pull her to me and claim her mouth, but I barely have time to taste her before she pushes me back.

"No!" She points a finger in my face. I suck it into my mouth and watch her eyes darken with lust. Her breasts heave with every intake of breath and she squirms in my lap. Her gaze never leaves my lips, she swallows hard, "No more kisses until you fix this."

I slide her finger out of my mouth with a wet *pop*. "Until *I* fix this? You cast the stupid curse. You fix it."

"I can't fix it, Mo. That's the whole point. Only you can break the curse, and to do that you'll have to tell the truth."

"I always tell the truth. Truth curse, remember?"

"Oh *puh*-lease." She rolls her eyes. "You lie all the time. I've known you long enough to know how Lucifer's curse works, and I know you only have to tell the truth if someone asks you a direct question. I also know how much you hate the curse which is why I always try to be as ambiguous as possible."

I open my mouth to refute her claims when I realise, she's right. Not just about Lucifer's curse—I worked that trick out less than five minutes after he slapped me with it— but about her ambiguity. I can't remember the last time she asked me something directly, well, besides her question from a few moments ago regarding the state of my heart, and the occasional, "Does my bum look big in these arse-less chaps?"

And all because she knows how much I hate my curse?

Wow. I'm... humbled? What does humble even feel like?

All I know is I want to please my woman, and the urge to do just that is pushing me hard. But without a stiff dick for her to ride, I have to explore other options.

Lifting her up and turning her around, I seat her back in my lap and tug her against my chest. Her skin is warm and soft, and she moans as she moulds herself to my large body. Her hair smells like water lilies, the soft strands tickling my chest.

Reaching for her breast with one hand and her pussy with the other, I slip two fingers inside her dripping cunt. Her small hand covers mine, encouraging me to delve deeper, thrust harder. Nuzzling my face into the crook of her neck, I kiss her hammering pulse, suck hard on her flesh and mark her as mine.

"I'm sorry. I can't give you what you want."

She seems to know I'm not talking about her pussy. Her voice is breathless, "What have you got to lose?"

"You, Nadia. I can't lose you."

Her hand reaches back for me, strokes my face. "You won't lose me, Mo."

She sounds so certain, but I know better. There's a reason I gave up trying to maintain long-term relationships with lovers. They always want what I can't give them— monogamy, fidelity, to be my one and only.

It never ends well.

"You know who I am. You know *what* I am. I need sex

to live, more sex than one lover can deliver. I can't be faithful to you, not without sacrificing what little soul I have left."

She's grinding down on my hand, moaning, so close to coming I can smell it in the air, feel it in the way her muscles quiver and clench. "I would never ask you to do that."

I whisper by her ear, "Then it's settled. Lift the curse, Nadia."

"Lift it yourself," she says, then screams in ecstasy as her pussy clamps down on my fingers and her body shakes in completion. Slumping against my chest, she pants as she tries to catch her breath, then slips from my lap and kneels between my legs. Taking my hand in hers, she lifts my pussy-soaked fingers to her mouth and sucks them one at a time between those pretty pink lips. "Three little words, Asmodeus. That's all it takes to lift your curse."

Watching her suck on my fingers, knowing she's licking her own flavour from them, is driving me crazy. I want her. I want to bury my cock deep in her pussy and thrust my tongue deep down her throat.

I want to shake off my human façade and take her as the demon she knows I am, big and bad and beautiful. I want to give her everything she wants, everything I am, everything I can never be. My heart, that blackguard, skips a beat at the thought of having her by my side for all eternity.

"Nadia."

My cock twitches.

Her eyes flare wide and zero in on the action. "I saw that. Whatever you were just thinking, think it again," she says, excitement lacing her tone. She leans farther into the space between my thighs, inspecting my cock as it dangles freely.

I swallow hard, excited, scared, aroused... but not enough.

Am I deluding myself, denying how I feel about her?

Twitch.

Would it really kill me to tell her I love her?

Twitch, twitch.

I know she deserves better, but what if I *could* make her happy?

Twitch, twitch, twitch.

I mean, it's been over four hundred years and she hasn't left me yet, right? Hasn't demanded my fidelity, hasn't asked me to be faithful. I'm not even sure she knows the meaning of the word *monogamy*. And even after all these years, she still surprises me, still excites me... still *loves* me.

Me!

The archdemon of lust, a prince of Hell, Asmodeus. I am sex and sin, lechery and desire. I am selfishness and wanton disregard for everyone's feelings but my own.

And hers.

She is my constant, my northern star, my little slice of Heaven on Earth. She is home. She *is* my heart.

Houston, we have lift-off.

After three months of little more than a good-for-nothing wet noodle in my pants, it feels good to fist my hand around an iron-hard cock. Nadia wastes no time in leaning forward to take me into her mouth, and as I fist a hand in her hair, I groan my pleasure. Her tongue is so soft, her teeth sharp and her mouth wet and warm, but it's not what I want.

Not what I need.

Easing her mouth off my cock, I bid her to stand and straddle me once more.

She stands before me, hands on hips, glorious in her

defiance. "Not until you say it." When I look down at my erection and then back at her, my brow raised, my grin cocky and my hint obvious, she hugs her arms around her waist and drops her gaze. "Please don't make me ask you."

So that's what this stupid curse has all been about. She wasn't jealous at all. She just wanted me to admit my love for her, and didn't want to use my curse to force the issue.

And it only took me three months to figure it out.

Well, four hundred years and three months.

I throw back my head and laugh at the irrationality of it all—me, the archdemon of lust, in love—then I stand and throw off my robe, my façade and the last of my objections. If this crazy chick wants to shackle herself to me for all time and all that entails, who am I to say no?

Towering over her in all my demonic glory, I brush a lock of hair from her face, stroke my fingers down her cheek. Taste the truth on the tip of my tongue. "Nadia, my little minx, I love you."

No sooner do the words leave my mouth than I feel something shift inside me, as if the shackles imprisoning my schlong have fallen away, released the beast. And three long months of sexual frustration claw at me, desperate for satis-faction.

Nadia throws her arms around my neck, her legs around my waist. "I love you, too."

I carry her to the bed, lay her down, and pin her hands above her head. She grins up at me and wiggles her enticing little body against mine. My balls draw up tight and my cock swells, ready to burst.

"Three months, my love. That's how long I've gone without sex. If you think you're getting out of this bed anytime soon, you can think again."

Parting her legs and tilting her pelvis, her body cradles my cock. "Bring it, big boy."

Fisting the base of my hard length, I tickle her clit with the rounded end of my dick, dip it down to her dripping cleft and then back to her clit again. Over and over until she's begging me to fill her up, begging me to fuck her, begging me to show her with my body what I've already told her in words.

I love her.

"You're killing me, Mo," she says with a throaty groan. "You're not the only one who's gone three months without sex, you know?"

She abstained while I suffered?

"You really do love me, don't you?"

Before she can answer, I take her mouth, slide my serpentine tongue inside that moist heat and taste her, make her so dizzy with lust that I won't be denied, then I slide my cock inside her cunt in one smooth thrust. She's hot and wet and tight, and I'm amazed I didn't blow my load the moment I entered her, but somehow I withstand the blinding, vice-like pressure of her pussy.

She mewls as I move inside her, as I slowly sink all the way into her. Too long my body has been denied the luxury of her silken heat, and I intend to take my time, savour every moment I'm inside her.

Letting go of her wrists, I trail my fingertips down her arms, around the curve of her breast and down her side to lift her leg around my waist. I rock my hips and push deeper inside her, her back arches and she moans her pleasure. Her fingernails score my back and I revel in the pain, in her passion.

I lock my gaze to hers and she doesn't shy away. The fathomless black depths of my eyes make lesser beings weep, but not her. Not my lover. Not only does she stare boldly back at me, but she pulls me down for another kiss, zealous and possessive. Then with a strength someone her size should not possess, she has me on my back and is riding me hard, my cock hitting so deep inside her pussy she screams her release like a demon horde riding into battle.

Barely does her orgasm subside before I lift her higher to sit on my face, urging her to ride my tongue as she rode my cock. She does, and it's glorious. Her scent, her flavour, her juices coat her thighs, my lips, my chin. Her hands grip my horns and hold me to her as she rides out another climax, as her sweet liquor runs over my tongue and down my throat.

She tastes like fine wine, ambrosia. She's better than fucking brandy.

And I want more.

I turn her around and thrust my hips towards her face.

She grabs my cock in one hand, my balls in the other. "Wine, dine, and sixty-nine. And here, I forgot to bring snacks."

I smack her arse and grin. *Cheeky bitch.* "Shut up and suck." And then I shove my face back in her snatch and go to town on her clit.

It takes her a moment to find her rhythm but once she does... *oh fuck!* She's an artist, her tongue the brush, my cock the canvas. But two can play at that game. Over and over I lave her pussy with my tongue, fuck her with my fingers, and probe that curvy arse. Again and again she screams her pleasure, again and again she comes and she comes.

Flipping her over, I take her from behind, hard and fast. Then I curl her in my arms and make love to her, slowly, thoroughly, and with a depth of feeling I never knew I owned. And then I'm on top of her again, her legs over my shoulders, hands pinned above her head and I'm slamming my cock deep inside her.

She feels so good, so hot and soft, so tight. My balls draw taut and I can't hold back. I feel her body quiver, hear her quickness of breath, see the flush in her cheeks, the glaze of lust in her eyes.

She's screaming. She's coming. And I am right there with her, every step of the way as the room vibrates with my roar of completion.

The smell of sex clings to our sweat slicked skin, surrounds us like fine perfume. I gather her close and stroke her hair, press a kiss to her forehead, and I know I made the right decision.

This woman is mine. She's been mine from the day I pulled her out of that stinking well, and she will be mine until the end of time.

My little naiad.

But....

It's time for the moment of truth. "I'm still hungry."

She rubs her face against the hard plane of my chest and yawns. "Then it's a good thing I called ahead and asked Jonathon to prepare you a late night snack," she said sleepily. "And by snack, of course, I mean orgy."

She sits up long enough to clap her hands loudly, the sound followed immediately by the doors being thrown open and a group of women, men and—*is that a satyr?*—following my valet into the room.

I'm about to open my mouth and give the sneaky bastard a piece of my mind when he has the audacity to wink at me. But when Nadia drapes herself over me and snuggles against my side, her warm breath brushing over my heated flesh and her contented sighs filling my heart with a long-forgotten joy, I cannot summon the will to punish him.

I settle for shooting him a sour glare, then turn my attention to my meal.

Taking my cock in hand, I watch the orgy unfold before me, watch as clothes are quickly discarded and the wondrous sounds of fucking, of breathy moans and balls slapping supple thighs fills the air around me.

Without the curse to shackle my life-force, the sexual energy filling the room permeates my very being until I am replete with it, until I'm bristling with power and shooting my load all over my hand. A pleasant languor seeps into my bones and I turn back to the goddess in my arms, watch as she dozes, hold her close and kiss her soft mouth.

After endless millennia alone, a life filled with lust and obsession, I never thought I'd fall in love. But now I have, I know I will never let her go. Nadia is my heart. My clever, bold, unpredictable heart. My woman. *Mine.*

And I am hers.

Always.

DIRTY LAUNDRY

For Danielle, for all the coffees shared and all the coffees yet to come.

Dirty Laundry

Fuck, fuck, fuckity fuck. Who the fuck is this guy and what the fuck is he doing in my happy place?

"My name is Adam, I'm doing my washing, and yes, you said that out loud."

Shit. "Sorry," I say with as much enthusiasm as I can muster, which admittedly at two in the morning isn't a great deal. He quirks an eyebrow at me, shakes his head and goes back to reading his book.

Double shit.

Head down, cheeks blazing and lips zipped, I drag my laundry duffel to the rear of the laundromat and fill two washing machines with a week's worth of dirty clothes and not-so-dirty sheets. I think I wash the sheets more out of habit than anything. I mean, it's not like I'm doing anything to make them unclean. I have no love life to speak of. There's no baby gravy to wash off or sex sweat to soak out. Nope. Nary an orgasm to be had in *my* bed.

Unless you count foodgasms. And meat sweats. And food babies.

God, I love food.

Almost as much as I love my local laundromat.

I love that it stays open twenty-four hours a day, seven days a week. I love that it has a coffee vending machine and, more to the point, the coffee doesn't taste like dirty mop water filtered through a sweaty jockstrap.

I love the enormous pink neon sign that stretches across the window and fills the shop with its ethereal glow. And I love that I can rock up at some ungodly hour of the morning and know without a doubt that I'll have the whole place to myself until sunrise, when the rest of the world suddenly awakens and fills up with people far more interesting than me.

At least that's how it usually goes.

Usually. But not tonight, apparently. Tonight I have to share the place with *Adam*.

Heaving a sigh, I set the machines to wash, then glance over at my interloper and his book. He's completely engrossed in whatever he's reading and not paying a lick of attention to me—not that anyone ever does—so I take a moment to soak up the sights.

Hey, if I have to share my happy place with the man, I may as well check him out.

Neatly trimmed brown hair and a clean-shaven face give him a well-groomed look, but a strong jaw, firm lips and a slightly crooked nose make him appear more rugged than pretty. His plain blue T-shirt hides his body, but the nicely sculptured biceps revealed by the short sleeves hint at a lean yet strong physique. His long legs are stretched out before him and crossed at the ankles, his jeans stretched taut by thighs thick with muscle.

He's yummy. He's dreamy. He's... the total opposite of every guy I've ever dated.

Let's face it, statistically speaking plain Janes like me

don't end up with men like, well, *him*. I mean, this guy looks like he exists on a diet of protein shakes and power bars and probably spends every available minute in the gym.

He's every jock in high school who made fun of my shapeless figure, every colleague who passed me over at the office Christmas party because my reputation for being a frigid bitch was apparently set in concrete.

In other words, he looks like a total dick.

Still, as dicks go he is handsome, and it's not likely he'll talk to me, absorbed in his book as he is.

Maybe this won't be such a chore after all.

With his face still buried in his book, I chance another look at those rock-hard thighs, sink my teeth into my bottom lip and imagine straddling—

"Are you going to stare at me *all* night?"

Shooting my gaze back to his face, I say, "What makes you think I'm staring at *you*?"

Watching me over the top of his book, he replies, "Baby, you ain't exactly subtle."

I cock a brow at the infantile nickname. "Baby? Do I look like a baby to you?"

Setting his book down on one solid thigh, his finger wedged between the pages to hold his place, he slowly peruses my body. I anchor my hands on my narrow hips and lift my chin, trying to ignore the sensual way his dark eyes roam over me.

And failing miserably.

My stomach flutters and my cheeks heat. The way he's watching me, I can almost feel his hands sliding under my clothes, over my skin, between my legs.... And I find myself trying *not* to remember the last time someone looked at me for so long without speaking. Gritting my teeth, I wait for the inevitable criticism.

Too tall, too thin, too boyish.

The usual complaints.

But after another lengthy moment of silently staring at each other, his lips lift at the corners in the slightest of grins. "No, ma'am. You look all grown up to me."

Wait. *What?*

No jokes about the itty-bitty titty committee? No backhanded compliments about my weight? No inappropriate eating disorder comments?

Huh.

Relieved and a little confused, I pull my shoulders back and narrow my gaze. "Then can you quit it with the 'baby' thing?"

He nods in deference and goes back to reading his book. "Sure thing."

"Thank you."

"Kitten."

I clench my jaw and glare at him, watch his grin broaden. I mutter under my breath, "Arse."

"Or you could just tell me your name," he says, then flicks over the page.

Obviously. I could do that. Or I could lie. "My name is Eve."

Adam puts his book down again and quirks an eyebrow. "Is this the part where I make a joke about you playing with my snake?"

A burst of laughter escapes me, blowing away the tension in the room. "Very funny."

"I thought so."

I put my duffel on a chair and walk over to the coffee machine. "Can I buy you a cup of coffee? An apology for swearing at you earlier."

His deep voice is mired in wariness. "Vending machine coffee?"

"Hey, don't knock it 'til you try it."

His lips twist, and for a moment I think he'll refuse, but then he says, "Black. One sugar."

Two minutes later, I hand him his coffee and take a sip of my own. "You know, research suggests that people who take their coffee black are psychopaths."

He watches me over the rim of his cup, the harsh glow of the fluorescent light above us reflecting off his dark green eyes. "The same could be said about people who do their laundry in the middle of the night."

"And here you're doing both," I say as I fold myself into the chair beside his. "And my real name is Georgia, by the way." I wrinkle my nose. "But everyone calls me George."

"Why?" he says, blowing on his coffee before taking a sip.

"Why what?"

"Why do they call you George?"

"You're kidding, right?" I shift in my chair and press my hand to my cheek to hide the prickling heat staining my face with colour, then take another sip of my flat white, as if that will magically make the situation less embarrassing.

He can't be that clueless.

Or maybe he thinks it's funny to make me admit my shortcomings out loud. He wouldn't be the first. I clear my throat and force myself not to swear at him again. "Some people think I look like a boy."

He tilts his head to stare at my chest. "Are these people blind? Because those are clearly breasts."

What started as a flush on my face and neck is now flooding my whole body with warmth. My nipples tighten into hard little peaks under my T-shirt, abrade against the cotton. A shiver of excitement skitters over my flesh, leaving a trail of goosebumps in its wake. *Is he flirting with me?* I play it cool. "And you clearly haven't seen me naked."

He gulps down his coffee and crushes the empty cup in his hand. "Actually, I have," he says, as though it's the most natural thing in the world to admit to a complete stranger that you've seen them in their birthday suit. "Twice." He shoots the scrunched-up cup like a basketball, wincing as it hits the rim of the rubbish bin and bounces to the floor. "So close."

He retrieves the cup and drops it in the bin, then leans against the bank of dryers on the wall opposite me, his eyes meeting mine, his gaze languid.

Adam has seen me naked?

Twice?

My breathing stutters and my mouth runs dry. Hoping a jolt of caffeine will snap my brain out of whatever fugue state it's in, I finish my coffee in record time. Maybe I misheard him? Maybe he's lying?

And maybe the grin he's wearing means no such luck. *Shit.* I misheard nothing.

Adam has seen me naked.

Twice.

Shoulders back and chin raised high, I ask, "How long have you been watching me?"

He folds his arms across his strong chest. "Long enough."

I do the math. I've been coming to this laundromat for six months. I got up the nerve to get my freak flag on about four months ago. The first time I dared to get naked was during my impromptu Bikram yoga session roughly five weeks ago, and the second time was last week when I....

Oh no.

I swallow hard and watch Adam with a wary eye, his smug grin telling me without a doubt what he saw.

Me. Here. Naked.

Masturbating.

Like, a lot.

"You're an exhibitionist."

His accusation leaves me breathless. He may as well have called me a slut. "I am not!"

Then why are my panties so very wet?

His smug grin has morphed into a simmering smile, and his dark eyes are fixed on mine, his focus unwavering, unnerving. "Okay, then what's with the Georgia Show every week? Why get naked if you don't want people to look at you?"

Arms crossed over my meagre chest and eyes narrowed, I stare him down. At least I try to. His dark, indolent gaze is unsettling. Like a predator tracking his prey, waiting for the right time to pounce.

And devour.

The world between us narrows, my awareness of Adam intensifies, focuses all my energy on not flinching under his intense scrutiny. I feel hot—*everywhere*. Pressing my thighs together, I try to ignore the slick heat pooling between my legs and hope I sound more confident than I feel as I shift in my chair.

"I don't get naked *every* week."

"No, you don't." He pushes away from the bank of dryers. "Week before last was your Jane Fonda workout, leg warmers and all." Another step closer. "Week before that, you had a roller disco. I could hear 'Dancing Queen' from across the street," he says, jerking his head towards the shop front and the empty street beyond the wall of neon lights and glass.

I push myself harder into the chair, pull my legs up in front of me like a protective shield as he provides proof that my weekly escapades have not gone as unnoticed as I'd believed.

My question is barely audible over the noise of the machines, and I hardly recognise the breathy sound of my own voice. "You could?"

"Mmhmm, and I'm not sure if it was the shorty-shorts, the Charlie's Angels T-shirt or the knee-high rainbow socks, but you looked so fucking sexy." He takes another step. "I'm not ashamed to admit it, Georgia. I jerked off while watching you."

Swallowing hard, I realise his admission should repulse me. It should be making me angry or scared, or at the very least grossed out. But I'm not. Instead, my skin prickles with heat and my pussy throbs. My gaze slides down his body from his rugged face to his strong arms, over his slim hips, and zeroes in on his crotch, on the—

Oh. *Wow!*

Enormous erection outlined in his jeans.

Holy shit. Eyes wide and breathing hard, I stare at his cock like I'm eyeing off fresh Danish, trying to imagine what it feels like in my mouth, what it tastes like.... The barrier of my legs relaxes and my feet slide off the chair and hit the floor. I sit forward and lick my lips.

"I like the way you think, kitten." Adam's voice rumbles through me and I watch, enthralled—*horrified*—as his hand reaches for his zipper.

My nerves catch fire and my muscles lock down, sweat beads at my temples.

What the fuck is happening here? For four months I've happily played dress-ups by myself and without interference. This is my safe space. The laundromat is my personal playground where I can be and do all the things I'm too chickenshit to be and do out there. In the real world.

Adam's not supposed to be here.

And I can't do this.

"Stop."

He does. He pauses for a split second before his hands detour to his pockets. The liquid heat of his dark eyes dims, takes on a cautious edge, and his face slips into an unreadable mask. He takes a step back, gives me space.

I fumble to explain. "I'm not who—*what*—you think I am."

"Oh?"

Shaking my head, my thoughts all jumble together. I'm confused, needy, wet, and the way his T-shirt clings to his broad shoulders and muscular biceps is making me really, really horny. But....

"I never meant for anyone to see me. I'm not like that. Not really. I mean,"—my voice drops to whisper—"why do you think I'm here at two in the morning? I'm a good girl. A boring girl, if you really want to know. I became an accountant, for fuck's sake, because I love maths. *Maths!* My nickname at work is Fifty Shades of Beige. I'm dull. I am wallpaper. And then you show up, and you're standing there looking all gorgeous and hot and telling me I'm sexy and staring at me like I'm the dirty girl of your wet dreams and I'm not." I hang my head. "I'm just... not."

Hot tears of frustration fill my eyes and I quickly dash them away. Adam steps closer, crouches down in front of me. His grin is gone, his smile smoothed out, his eyes focused on mine, staring at me like I'm a puzzle he's determined to solve.

"So let me see if I understand what you're trying to say.

There are *two* Georgias? The boring girl you actually are, and the dirty girl you pretend to be?"

Relief forces air to explode out of my lungs and I nod. *He gets it.* "Yes. Thank you, yes."

But—*uh-oh*—that grin is back. "And it never occurred to you that maybe, just maybe, the dirty girl is who you really are and the boring girl is who you pretend to be?"

Wait. "What?"

"Do you know what you were doing the first time I saw you?"

Wondering what depraved thing he'll announce he saw me doing this time, I rub my suddenly sweaty palms on my jeans. "No."

"You were reading a book. That's all. You were sitting right here, just like you are now, and you were reading a book."

Brows pulling together, I stare at him, suspicious of where this conversation is going. "You realise you're proving *my* point, right?"

"I don't think so. I think perhaps what you think is *boring* you is actually just *quiet* you. Because I refuse to believe the girl who plays air guitar on a tabletop while belting out 'Eye Of The Tiger' is boring."

Annnd just when I thought I couldn't blush any more tonight.... "You saw that too?" Groaning in embarrassment, I bury my face in my hands, my cheeks burning. But I peek through my fingers when I hear his rumbling chuckle of laughter. I see that sexy grin of his and my insides clench.

He answers with an unapologetic smirk. "Yep."

"Oh, God. Is there anything you didn't see?"

His gaze drops to my breasts, his dark eyes intense once more. "I know there are a few things I'd like to see again."

"And what, you think I'm just going to whip them out for you to play with?"

Adam stands and grins down at me. "Yes, I do. Because whether you want to admit it or not, Georgia, you are an exhibitionist. Maybe only when you think other people aren't watching, but that doesn't mean you don't want to be seen." He holds out his hand and waits patiently until I reach out and take it. Pulling me to my feet, he grips my chin and stares into my eyes, making sure I can't look away. Voice soft and low, he says, "I see you, kitten."

Barely containing a whimper of arousal, I bite my lip. He tilts his head, leans down to kiss me, but I step back and out of his grasp. "What if...?" I swallow hard and try again. "What if...?"

Warm hands settle on my shoulders, gently massage the tightness and the tension I always seem to carry. I can't help but lean into him, feel his heat, his strength. His massive erection. "What's wrong?"

Before I can stop them, the words I've been searching for tumble free. "I don't know if I can do this."

Adam stiffens a little, taken aback as if the possibility I might reject his advances never occurred to him. Not that I am rejecting him, exactly.

But I need to be sure.

"What I mean is, mucking around on my own is one thing, but what if...?" I ignore every impulse telling me to throw myself at this man, to grab what he's offering with both hands and run with it. I straighten my back and hope my voice doesn't waver. "What if I say no?"

His chest rises and falls with measured breaths, his eyes almost black. "I don't get off on assaulting women, if that's what you're worried about. If you want me to go, I'll go," he says, then drops his gaze to my lips. He leans a little closer, whispers his words across my cheek, layers them with meaning. "But if you want me to stay...."

In other words, I'm in control.

I search his eyes for an eternity, looking for the hidden joke, waiting for the other shoe to drop, for the streamers and balloons to explode down from the ceiling and some horrible, gaudy game show host to jump out laughing, "Gotcha!" But I see nothing, no one. Just Adam watching me with narrowed eyes, his cautious expression at odds with the lust and the longing—the *hope*—I see smouldering in his dark green depths.

He wants me.

Me!

A single word whispers past my lips. "Stay."

His mouth is on mine in an instant, his lips firm and hot, and that whimper I've been suppressing finally escapes me as I kiss him back. Running my fingers through his hair, I fist my hands in the short strands and hold him to me. He groans and pushes his mouth against mine, harder, more urgent. Then suddenly he's pulling back and yanking his T-shirt over his head, tossing it on the floor.

My mouth runs dry at the sight of him. That sneaky T-shirt was hiding a goldmine of drool-worthy abs wrapped in soft skin.

So fucking lickable.

I glance up at his face, then back to that fit chest, back to all that hard muscle and tanned skin. I want him. With a tentative hand, I reach out and touch him, afraid he's not real, that the fumes from the budget-friendly fabric softener I use have finally scrambled my brain and I'm actually hallucinating, but my fingertips meet with hot, solid flesh.

Oh, he's real, all right.

Really hard, really smooth and really fucking sexy.

I splay my hands over his chest and explore the expanse of him, finger each ridge of muscle, trace the outline of his nipples and watch them pucker into hard brown peaks. Leaning forward, I take one between my teeth and gently pull at it.

A hissing sound escapes him as he sucks in his breath, followed by a low moan and a whispered "Fuck" when I swirl my tongue around it and suck it between my lips.

"You like that, baby?"

He angles me back against the table in the centre of the room, his mouth latched around my earlobe. "Oh, so I'm baby now. I see how it is," he says with a laugh.

I grin. "You don't like baby, baby?"

"Baby works for me, kitten." And then he's nibbling a line along my jaw and down my neck, licking the hollow at the base of my throat where my collarbones meet.

I slide my hands all over his chest and shoulders and —*holy shit*—those biceps. There's just so much of him. So much muscle, so much strength and heat. The pure male-ness of him is impressive. Beyond compare.

"You like what you see, kitten?"

Do I *like* what I see? Words fail me, and the noise that leaves my mouth as I nod my approval is part whimper, part sigh, and sounds about as dignified as a cat in heat. I want, I crave. A primal urge to claim him as mine has me biting him again, scoring his pectoral muscle with my teeth. He yelps at my roughness.

I lick and kiss the welt I left on his skin. "Sorry, it's just I've never seen a man like you before. Not like this, not up close and personal. You're..." I lick my lips, eager for another taste. "You're magnificent."

"And you're a little too good for my ego." He pulls me to him for another passionate kiss, his tongue pushing into my mouth and flicking against my own. He moans as he pulls back. "Your turn. Shirt. Off."

Butterflies swirl in my belly as I reach for the hem of my T-shirt and slowly lift it up. I'm not wearing a bra. Why bother? I mean, I'm not completely flat-chested, but I'm not exactly winning any wet T-shirt contests anytime soon either. But Adam watches me with a rapt expression that fuels my ego and settles the fluttering in my gut. Even so, history has taught me to be cautious, and I slow my movements.

Big hands slide around my hips. Adam growls, his fingers flex and grip. Eager. Impatient. "You're killing me, kitten."

I lift my head and look up at him as his tongue darts out to moisten his lips, as his chest heaves with every intake of breath. His gaze is glued to my breasts as if he's waiting for the curtain to rise on the most exciting show in the world.

He's going to be disappointed.

I decide the Band-Aid approach is best. Just rip it off and see what happens. And with one quick tug, my shirt is off. It dangles from my fingertips, ready to be whipped up in front of me, to cover the little ladies should things go sideways. But as I feel his fingers tighten on my hips, as I hear his breath catch and exhale on a shuddering sigh, my T-shirt slips from my fingers and out of my reach.

"They're perfect," Adam says, leaning down to kiss each one in turn, taking his time to lick and suck each of my sensitive nipples until they stand erect and proud. He lifts his face to meet mine. "You're perfect."

My breath stutters in my chest. Perfect? I would have been happy if he thought I was mediocre, above average even. But *perfect*?

This guy is getting the ride of his fucking life tonight!

Scrambling for the button at his waist, my urgency matches his as he reaches for the belt buckle at mine. Our mouths crash together, jerky and laughing as we strip each other of the last of our clothes, kick off our shoes and tug off our socks.

Adam lifts me onto the table's edge, wraps one big arm around my waist and roughly shoves my legs apart, settles his hot body between my knees, then leans over me until I'm lying almost flat. His mouth latches around one pert pink nipple, sucks hard and pulls my breast upwards until it can go no farther, then lets it go and grins as it bounces against my chest. Over and over he does this, one breast and then the other, back and forth, driving me crazy as glorious tension flows through me, an electric pulse that shoots from my breasts to my pussy and then pinballs back to my brain. My poor throbbing brain, consumed with one burning question.

"Why didn't you talk to me sooner?"

His lips twist into a self-deprecating smile. "You're not the only one who hides in plain sight."

"What do you mean?"

Resting his weight on his forearm, he toys with my hair, sifts the long dark strands through his fingers and watches them fall around me as he speaks. "I'm the night manager at the supermarket two blocks that way," he says, nodding towards the back wall of the laundromat. "And I live one block that way." A jerk of his head towards the front window. "I can't remember the last time I did anything, went anywhere beyond these three city blocks. Home, work, home, work—and then I saw you. I was just walking home from work one night and saw a pretty girl reading a book. I wanted to talk to you, but I didn't know how. And then I saw you again the next week. And the next." He takes a deep breath, as if bracing himself for what he says next, or guarding himself against my reaction to it. "I've watched you for so long. Wanted you for so long."

I smile, a big puffed-up grin that stretches from cheek to cheek. Fifty Shades of Beige, my arse. I know I should be scared, that Adam's words should terrify me—I mean seriously, stalker much?—but I'm not, and they don't. Maybe he's right. Maybe I am a dirty girl, because knowing he was across the street, watching me, waiting, wanking... I feel... *alive*. Excited. And so very turned on.

Every nerve in my body bursts with energy. And the way he's looking at me, like I'm the only thing anchoring him to the planet.

I feel needed.

I feel powerful.

His hips flex between my legs, and he pushes his hard cock against the slick folds of my pussy. His groan echoes mine as I yank him down to kiss me.

"Enough with the watching. Enough with the waiting. I want you inside me, and I want you now."

In the time it takes to issue my demand, he thrusts inside me, then stills. His cock is so big, so thick, and he's stretching me open. *Shit*. I haven't had a dick this big since... ever.

"*Sooo* wet." Adam moans long and loud. "Fuck, your body is tight. Must be all that yoga," he says with a wink.

Wicked laughter bubbles up from inside me. "Shut up and fuck me."

He pumps his hips. "Anything you want, kitten."

Thrusting slowly, he lowers himself over me and teases me with kisses, swooping in and pulling back, making me chase him, making me giggle. Making me fucking *giggle*! Then he tongues my breasts again. Sucks and nips at my sensitive buds until I want to scream, back and forth and over and over until the knot in my belly begins to unravel and I feel like I'm burning up, intense heat exploding outwards through my limbs, blinding me to everything around us.

Everything but him.

The softness of his lips, the bite of his teeth, the heat of his tongue.

I'm coming. I'm coming hard as his unhurried thrusts and masterful mouth push me over the edge and into a sensual oblivion.

My gaze roams freely over his face and body as I recover, studying every contour, memorising every feature. A small scar adorns the bridge of his nose, the skin there paler than the rest of him. His eyes, a green so dark they're almost black, soft and rich like the finest velvet. His body, his wonderful, powerful body, is sleek steel covered in satin, smooth and hot and hard. Sliding my hands over his chest and along his arms, I feel his muscles bunch and quiver as he thrusts deep inside me.

"I love watching you come." His voice is so deep, the sound heady as he talks dirty to me. "When I watched you last week," he says, his hips rocking to their own careful rhythm, "when you were here on this table with your head dangling over the end and staring straight through the window... oh, shit." His eyelids flutter, he shivers. "You were staring right at me, kitten. And the look on your face when you came...." Another shiver. "*Bliss*."

"Did you come too?" I say, panting like a bitch in heat, his gentle thrusting driving me crazy with need, pushing me to the edge of my next orgasm. "Did you come with me?"

Palming my breast, he squeezes hard. "Yes. Fuck yes."

I arch up into his hand, his skin hot, his fingers

calloused. "Will you come with me now?"

Adam laughs, the sound warm and welcome by my ear. "You are such a dirty girl."

I bite my lip and grin. "You like me 'cause I'm dirty."

"Yeah, I do." He speeds up his movements, thrusting into me with such force the table begins to squeak in protest, its metal feet scraping over the linoleum floor.

My orgasm builds, just as volatile, just as intoxicating as the first. Adam slips an arm under me, forcing my pelvis to tilt. His cock sinks deeper, and we both groan. Sucking air into my lungs in great gulps, I try not to pass out from the passion he's wringing from my body.

Pussy clenching.

Muscles quivering.

"Come with me, baby. Come with me." And then I'm falling, ripples of delicious pleasure cascading through me as my orgasm hits. "Adam!" I claw at his shoulders and biceps.

Staring up at his face, I watch his jaw drop, his eyes close, and then he's pulling his cock from inside me and spilling his come on my belly.

Marking me with his seed.

Taking my hands in his, he helps me sit up, then kisses me long and slow.

I run my fingers through his come and smooth it over my skin like an exotic lotion.

"Fuck, that's hot," he says, a quiet growl sounding deep in his throat.

Looking down at his softening cock, I lick my lips.

I want to know what he tastes like.

Slipping from the table, I gather our clothes and kneel at his feet. He smiles down at me and slides his fingers into my hair, fists the strands at the back of my skull.

"Kitten," he murmurs, the word little more than a breathy groan.

The sound sends a little shiver through me, spurs me into action.

With my hands anchored on his strong thighs, I lean forward and take him in my mouth. He exhales a faltering breath. The last few droplets of his come blend with the flavour of my pussy and coat the tip of my tongue—rich and sweet and salty. I swirl my tongue around the head of his cock and suck him deep down my throat. He moans his approval and sinks his other hand into my hair to join the first, guiding me as I slide my lips up and down his hardening shaft.

Adam's eyelids droop, and his mouth falls open. "Georgia." The reverence in his voice as he breathes my name fills me with such warmth that I can't help but smile—well, as much as I can with his cock in my mouth. Primal need quickly replaces his adoration, and he thrusts his hips, fucks my face, but just when I think he'll choke me on his giant cock, he forces me to my feet and drags me to the window.

Spinning me to face the street, his voice is urgent, commanding. "Brace your hands on the glass, kitten."

Ignoring the command, I turn back and lean into him, rake my fingernails over his abs and kiss a path heading down. "But I was enjoying sucking your cock."

He yanks me back up, smacks my arse and shoves me towards the window once more. "Do it. Now."

I pout. "Why?"

Brushing my hair aside, he whispers in my ear. "Because I want everyone to see how fucking beautiful you are when you come all over my dick."

I brace my hands on the window and stare at our reflection, our skin glowing pink under the neon sign that stretches over our heads. "Everyone?" A frisson of panic—of *excitement*—shivers through me.

"Oh, Georgia." Adam's reflection smiles back at me, a wicked gleam in his eyes as his fingers dig into my hips and he slides inside my pussy, sinking into my wet heat with a masculine groan. "You didn't really think I was the only one out there, did you, kitten?"

Eyes wide, I try to see who's outside the laundromat. Adam chuckles, his laughter reverberating through my body as easily as the shock waves from his thrusting hips. With one hand holding me in place, he reaches under me to play with my clit, and suddenly I'm not wondering if anyone is out there anymore. Suddenly my focus is all on the man I know is in here. Behind me. Inside me. Our bodies slapping together with increasing force as he takes me from fantasy to reality as easily as flicking a switch.

Speaking of flicking switches....

The combination of Adam's cock in my pussy and his fingers on my clit pushes me ever closer to another orgasm. He pulls me upright, and I gasp as he pushes my body flush against the window, the force of his thrusting and the chill of the glass overstimulating my already-sensitive nipples. "Adam. Baby." My panted breaths fog the glass.

"I've got you, kitten." He nuzzles the back of my neck, kisses and licks and sucks my flesh, adding to the sensations ricocheting around my body like a bullet. Pussy. Breasts. Clit. Neck. Hips. Pussy. Clit.

Everything is spinning out of control.

"Baby, please, I'm going—I'm going to come."

"Come for me, Georgia. Let them see." Then he lifts my leg, hooks his arm under my knee and opens me wide for any prying eyes to witness. "Show them how beautiful you are."

"Adam, yes!"

My body undulates between him and the window, rattling the glass with the force of my orgasm. Barely a moment passes before Adam is right there with me, thrusting like a wild man and slamming himself into me like his life depends on it, crying out as he spills himself inside me. And as my orgasm slowly subsides, as my heart slows and my breathing calms, I can feel our passion trickle down my thighs.

So dirty.

So *free*.

Adam pulls out of me and turns me in his arms, holds me close and strokes my hair. And we just stand there, sweaty, sticky and naked in the middle of an all-night laundromat.

The strangeness of the situation is underscored by the beeping of the washing machines as they finish their cycles. Our bodies shake with quiet laughter, the sound one of familiarity, of comfort. Of warmth. And that's how the rest of the evening passes.

In the warmth of each other's arms, talking, fucking.

Reading books and folding laundry.

But now the sun is rising, its golden glow reflecting off the glass and steel of the buildings up and down the street, casting shadows across the concrete and the bitumen.

The real world encroaches.

It's time for us to go.

I avoid Adam's gaze as I finish dressing and finger comb my hair. "So... same time next week?" I bite my lip, my foot bouncing as I await his answer.

Hefting his laundry bag over his shoulder, he says, "No. I don't think so."

While not completely unexpected, his rejection stings.

All the things he said, the things we did and—oh, God—the things we *didn't* do. Like use protection. *Fuck.* I've never behaved so wild, so recklessly in all my life. But I thought... I thought—

Georgia, you fucking idiot. What did you think would happen?

Stupid, stupid, stupid Georgia.

With self-recrimination coursing through my blood, I force myself to breathe, to shove down my hurt and disappointment. "Oh."

Back straight and body tense, I grab my bag and head for the door, but I can't get past the wall of muscle blocking my way. Tears burn behind my eyes, threatening to fall.

Hooking a knuckle under my chin, Adam lifts my face to his. "Please don't cry, kitten," he murmurs, then wipes an errant tear from my cheek. His mouth is curved in a lopsided smile that lacks the cockiness from last night. "I only meant that I don't—no, that I *can't* wait that long to see you again."

My heartbeat flutters, I suck in a lungful of air. Another flutter, and a smile slowly stretches my lips. One I can't stop. Couldn't even if I wanted to. And my voice sounds less wooden as I repeat myself, "*Oh.*"

He pushes the door open, and we step out into the chill of the dawn. "There's a great café on the bottom floor of my apartment building. They do an all-day breakfast... if you're hungry?"

Great sex *and* he wants to feed me? I swallow down a contented sigh. "Are they open this early?"

"Nope." He slips his hand into mine and gives it a squeeze. "But I'm sure we can find something to do until then."

I glance down at our intertwined fingers and cock one

brow. "Oh yeah? Like what?"

We cross the street and head in the direction of his apartment. "Did I ever tell you my dining room window overlooks the park?"

I bite back a grin. "Is that a fact?"

"Mmhmm. And at this time of day there's bound to be loads of joggers, dog walkers.... Hell, anyone could wander by and look up."

I laugh. "You're just a dirty old man, aren't you?"

He drops his laundry bag and pulls me in for a toe-curling kiss, a hot, languid promise of more to come. "You like me 'cause I'm dirty," he says, throwing my own words back at me with a wink. "And I'm not that old." Then he grabs his bag and we start walking again.

Yeah, I like Adam because he's dirty. I like him more because he makes me feel extraordinary, accepted. *Seen.* I'm not wallpaper anymore.

I am Georgia, and I'm kitten. I'm quiet, and I'm sexy. I'm a good girl and an exhibitionist.

I am *not* boring.

If the last four months have taught me anything, it's that I am whatever the fuck I want to be. Right now, seeing the naughty glint in Adam's dark eyes, the way he's looking at me like I'm his wet dream come to life....

All I want to be is dirty.

SANTA CLAUS IS COMING

For Nelly, the other cougar in my life.

Santa Claus Is Coming

"Please tell me that was the last one."

Holly grins at me. "That was the last one."

"Thank God." I push myself up and out of the driftwood throne I've occupied for the better part of the day and stretch the kinks out of my back and shoulders.

Everything hurts.

My back is stiff from sitting for too long, and my thighs hurt from having an endless line-up of kids—and the occasional adult—sit on them all day. My cheeks ache from smiling *waaay* too much, my arse is so numb I'm not entirely sure it's still attached to my body, and don't even get me started on the state of my balls....

Fuck me.

What a day.

When my best friend's sister invited me to spend the day with her at Melbourne's iconic Brighton Beach—you know the one, with the long line of brightly painted bathing huts that wedding photographers clamour over—I jumped at the opportunity. Spend the day with the woman I've lusted after for years while she parades around in one of those skimpy bikinis she's so fond of?

Fuck yeah!

And sure, maybe I could catch a few waves while we're there, show off my very grown-up, non-brotherly physique to the woman who once told me *a*) she'd never date one of her brother's mates, and *b*) she'd never, ever be interested in someone so much younger than her.

Like a ten-year age difference made her old or something.

Women!

Anyway, I rock up, surfboard in hand, and what does she do? Hands me a beach bum Santa costume consisting of little more than a pair of boardshorts and a Santa hat, shoves me in front of a camera and starts charging people money to let their precious little darlings crawl all over me and tell me their Christmas wishes.

Which okay, crushed ball-sack aside, it was actually pretty cool, especially the kid who wanted total world domination so he could end bullying everywhere. I didn't have the heart to point out the flaw in his plan, and judging by the look on his dad's face, neither did he.

"You did a good job today, Christopher," Holly says as she packs away her camera equipment, then laughs. "I can't wait to show Mikey that shot of the granny in your lap."

I slip off my Santa hat and shove it in my pocket. "I'll have you know her name was Phillipa. She's seventy-five years young, and she said I reminded her of her late husband."

"She licked your face."

"Apparently she wanted to know if I tasted like him, too," I say with a grin. "I reckon the saucy old dame did it to win a bet, actually. I saw her and her friend exchange a tenner after she collected her photo. And you know Mike hates it when you call him Mikey, right?"

"Of course. Why do you think I do it?" she says with a wink that makes my breath stall in my chest and my legs go weak at the knees. "Seriously, though, thanks for today. I know I blindsided you with it."

"You know, you could've just told me what you wanted me for," I say as I step down from the dais and discreetly adjust my aching package. "It *is* for charity. And you know us firemen. We love any excuse to take our shirts off."

She looks up at me from under long, thick eyelashes. "After the calendar shoot fiasco, I wasn't sure how willing you'd be to help me."

Ah, yes. The calendar fiasco. I snort a laugh and shake my head. "I run into burning buildings for a living, Hols. On purpose. Did you really think a little dog shit would keep me away?"

Holly laughs, the full-bodied sound bursting from within her and shaking her deliciously plump figure with the force of it.

Good God, I want to eat her all up. Starting right between her—

"It was more than a *little* dog shit," she says, the reminder killing my burgeoning erection. "That poor pup had the worst diarrhoea I've ever seen. You were covered in it. I have photos. I was thinking of blowing one up and giving it to your mum for Christmas."

Cocking an eyebrow at her obvious glee, I fold my arms over my chest and grin. "You just love humiliating me, don't you?"

"Call it a hobby," she says with a shrug, her pretty mouth curved in a smile of honest good humour. A smile that has my cock twitching to life again as I imagine how those sweet lips would feel wrapped around its rock-hard length.

Fuck.

The last thing I need right now is a hard-on. I'm almost thankful for the sudden wind that whips past us, stinging my legs with flying sand.

Looking out over the bay, the darkening clouds are swallowing the blue sky and sunshine like a ravenous beast. How the hell didn't I notice a storm that big sneaking up on us? Holly's bikini and see-through kaftan combo probably has something to do with it. But damn, that thing is moving fast and heading inland. Towards us.

I look up and down the beach, watching people packing away their gear and hurrying up their kids, trying to make it back to their cars before the rain hits. "Looks like we're in for one hell of a storm. Let's get this stuff packed up. Where do you want it?"

A rumble of thunder has Holly looking skyward. A burst of bright blue lightning has her unceremoniously shoving the last of her gear in her bag and hauling arse towards the nearest bathing box.

"Over here."

Flinging the doors open on the little timber shed, she puts her bag on the old daybed inside, then runs back to help me dismantle the driftwood throne and the small dais it sits on.

"When did you get a box?" I ask as we carry the various bits and pieces to the tiny hut and stack them inside.

"As if I could afford one of these," she says with a snort, going back for the inflatable kangaroos she pegged to the sand. "It belongs to a client. I shot his portrait here last year, and I always thought it would be a great spot for a Summer Santa photo op. Anyway, Mal's spending the holidays with family up north this year, so he gave me permission to use it while he's away."

An irrational flare of jealousy makes my jaw tighten and my stomach clench. Who is this *Mal* she knows so well he would lend her the use of his bathing box—a privilege usually reserved for family members only—and why do I suddenly want to rip his fucking head off?

Small droplets of rain splash against my skin, distracting me from my wayward thoughts. The temperature drops and a sudden chill skates over my half-naked body, making me wish I was wearing something more than just a pair of Christmas-themed boardshorts.

Another rumble of thunder sounds overhead, louder this time.

Closer.

Then the storm starts in earnest, a downpour pelting us with cold, stinging rain, the heavy drops of water leaving tiny craters in the sand at our feet.

I look over at Holly. She's tossed two kangaroos inside the box and gone back for the third. I stack the last panel from the portable dais, then pause to glance at her again. She seems to have everything well in hand, so I grab my surfboard and beach bag and shove them inside too. No way I'm trudging all that shit back to my car in this kind of weather.

Just as I'm dusting the last of the sand off my hands and pushing my wet hair out of my eyes, I hear more thunder, see more lightning, and then—

A bang.

A scream.

"Holly!"

Years of emergency response training flies out the window as I run towards her, towards a hazard I know nothing about with no more course of action in my head beyond *Save Holly*.

Stopping short of my target, my heart leaps at the sight of her, a crumpled heap on the ground with her arms flung over her head, her clothes soaked through and stuck to her lush body, offering her no protection as the wind and rain lash her pale, lifeless flesh.

My heart stops beating and my voice is a whisper of breath, forcing itself past the lump in my throat. "No."

But then her leg twitches, and my heart jams back into overdrive, forcing my body to move, to rush to her side. *Save. Holly*. Skidding in the wet sand, I kneel beside her. Sending up a silent prayer of thanks, I search her body for injuries, run my hands over her, look for anything out of place, then coax her into sitting up so I can see her face.

"It popped," she says, her voice quiet, shaky.

I glance at the inflatable kangaroo. It's slumped over and deflating fast, air escaping its big fake carcass through a massive hole in the side of its head and an ugly black gash that's melted into its body. Noting the string of small metal bells tied around its neck, the metal tent peg she used to anchor the bloody thing to the ground, and the jagged clumps of hardened sand surrounding the metal peg, my teeth clench and I curse under my breath.

Metal.

The lightning must've hit it.

Fuck.

I stare at Holly and a fist squeezes around my heart. This could've been so much worse.

Mixed emotions rage inside me. On the one hand I'm grateful she's alive, while on the other I want to wring her bloody neck for being so careless. But neither emotion is useful right now, not when I need to take care of her.

Holly's hair is plastered to her face and neck, and I gently push it aside. Cupping her cheeks, I stare into her eyes. Clenching my jaw, I force myself to ignore their brilliant blue colour and focus on her pupils instead.

"Are you hurt?" She's not listening, her eyes dancing back and forth. I have to get her inside and out of this shit weather, but I have to make sure she isn't hurt first. The last thing she needs is for me to move her the wrong way and make any injuries worse. "Holly. Focus." I use my bossy voice, the one I reserve for trainees and casualties who've descended into shock. Calm but commanding. "Are you hurt?"

Her gaze finally focuses on my mine, her pupils dilating. Good. She's responsive. "What?"

I slick her hair back, and she blinks the rain out of her eyes. "I said, are you hurt?"

Another crack of lightning makes her flinch towards me, into the circle of my arms. Somehow I resist the urge to crush her to my chest.

"No, not hurt."

"You're sure?"

"Yes."

"Good." In one easy, practiced move, I lift her over my shoulder and run back to the bathing box. Putting her back on her feet, I say, "Get inside and get out of those wet clothes."

I follow her inside and shut the doors behind us, plunging us into darkness.

"Hey! I can't see."

"You don't need the lights on to take your clothes off."

Holly grumbles something under her breath about my attitude problem, but I'm too busy groping around in the dark to pay her much attention.

This would be so much easier if I could just switch on a light, but in keeping with their Victorian heritage, the bathing boxes don't have electricity. No windows either. Finally finding what I'm searching for, I retrace my steps until I find my bag, then dig around for my kit.

My eyes slowly adjust to the gloom of the bathing box, making it slightly easier to find what I'm looking for. Still, I'm flying almost blind when I strike a match and cradle the tiny flame in the palm of my hand, but a moment later....

"Let there be light." The flat cotton wick flickers to life, brightening as I lower the glass bulb into place. "I saw this old kero lamp tucked in the corner when I was stacking this stuff," I say, nudging the driftwood with my foot. Noticing a hook anchored to the rafter above the daybed, I hang the lamp and look down at Holly, still standing by the bed, dripping water all over the floor and shivering in her soaked clothes. "I thought I told you to get undressed."

My words come out sharper than I intend, but screw it.

I'm pissed off.

With the lamp above our heads, I can see her face again. See her determined scowl and fierce eyes, her flattened mouth and the stubborn lift of her dimpled chin.

She plants her hands on her hips. "I'm not a child, Chris. You can't just boss me around like one of your newbies."

A muscle ticks in my cheek. "Maybe not. But last I checked, I am the only emergency services personnel within cooee of the place who has advanced first aid training, and if we don't get out of these wet clothes and start getting warmed up, we'll be in for a seriously shit afternoon."

She snorts at me. "You mean it could get worse?"

"It almost was worse," I snap, my irritation no longer willing to take a back seat to my forced civility.

She straightens and her brows pull together. "Why are you so angry? I told you, I'm fine."

I roll my shoulders, but the tension that's been riding me since I heard her scream just won't shift. I want to throttle her for making me so worried. "Fine? Do you have any idea how badly that could've ended? What the hell were you thinking, Holly? A metal tent peg in a lightning storm?"

"How was I supposed to know some freak storm would blow up out of nowhere? There was nothing about it in the weather reports last night."

I grind my teeth. "Did you check the reports this morning?"

She shrugs. "No."

My hands clench and my voice drops. "Are you fucking kidding me?"

She's watching me, her eyes narrowed, her voice strident. "No, I'm not fucking kidding you, Chris. Look, I know it could've been worse, but it wasn't. So just drop it, okay?"

"No, it's not okay." I shove my hands through my hair to stop myself from grabbing her and let loose an exasperated sigh, reminding myself she's just a civilian. She hasn't witnessed first-hand the devastation a sudden change in the weather can wreak. The utter destruction of people's homes, their livelihoods.

Their lives.

"One second, Hols. That's all it would've taken. If you'd been one second slower—" I can't even finish voicing the thought, not without completely losing my shit. Hearing her piercing scream, seeing her lying there, an unmoving heap on the ground....

Fuck. I thought I was over her. I honestly thought all I felt for her now was lust, nothing but desire and hunger.

Boy, was I wrong.

My muscles tense as she gently lays one hand on my arm, cupping my cheek with the other. Her tone is as soft as her skin, and I fight the urge to lean into her palm.

"Chris, look at me. I'm fine. I'm cold and I'm wet, but I'm whole."

The chill of her flesh on mine wakes up the more rational parts of my brain. "Then do as you're told and take off your clothes." I don't wait to see if she obeys. I find my bag and dig out a dry pair of shorts, a T-shirt, and a beach towel. "Does your *friend* keep any blankets or towels in here?" I ask as I shuck my wet boardshorts and kick them across the floor. When she doesn't answer, I ask again. "Holly?"

I turn around and see her standing there, shirt off, bikini on, nipples hard and clearly visible through the red triangles of fabric attempting to contain her large breasts and almost succeeding. I take a deep breath and force my eyes up to her face.

What is she staring at?

Her throat bobs. "You're naked."

"So?" I toss the towel at her. "It's not like you've never seen me naked before." When she continues to stand there, staring at me, her gaze wandering slowly over my body, her teeth sinking into the lush pillow of her bottom lip, I fold my arms across my chest, cock one brow, and say, "Do you need a hand?"

She whips the towel up in front of her. "No. I've got it, thanks. And blankets. Yes. In the box under the bed."

Nudging her out of the way, I retrieve the well-worn woollen blankets, then hand her my T-shirt and give her my back while I step into my spare boardshorts.

"Um, you don't have any undies in that bag, do you?"

Turning, I fight back a grin—I'm not quite finished being mad at her yet. "Nope. Why? Is there a problem?"

Holly glares at me, presses her thighs together, and yanks on the bottom of the T-shirt, stretching it south in a bid to cover her naked pussy. "Yes, Chris. There's a problem. You might be bigger than me, but my boobs are bigger than yours and they're stopping your shirt from coming down far enough to cover my—" She clears her throat. "—privates."

"Do you want to swap?"

She makes an irritated sound in the back of her throat, and I can practically see the cogs turning in her head, imagining me in the T-shirt with my dick hanging out and her in my shorts with her rack on display. Through clenched teeth, she says, "No. I want underwear."

"Sorry," I say with a shrug. "But I don't wear undies unless I'm working, and even then it's under duress. Same goes for shaving and cutting my hair. So it's a good thing for you I'm on leave or your Santa would've been beardless."

She continues glaring at me. "I'd hardly call that scruff a beard."

I shake my head. "Just get under the blanket."

Answering the command with pursed lips and another little growl, I can see her reluctance to let go of the shirt, to let it spring back to its usual length and reveal her *privates*. The glow of the lamp is too dull to see if she's blushing, but I can imagine, and this time I let my grin come to the surface.

Making her uncomfortable is easing my temper.

Just a bit.

"Fine," she snaps and turns her back on me. She bends down to grab a blanket off the bed, granting me a fantastic view of her long, shapely legs and luscious, rounded arse in the process.

And just a peek of her pretty pink pussy.

Fuck. Me.

I tilt my head to get a better look. Big mistake. My pants suddenly become very uncomfortable, my erection pitching the brightly coloured polyester like a fucking circus tent. I turn away before she sees.

Crouching down, I dig through my bag and pull out my Jetboil mini stove, two bottles of water, and a packet of Cup-a-Soup.

Behind me, the daybed squeaks as Holly shifts about. "Do you want a blanket?"

I hand her a bottle of water, then empty the other into the Jetboil's billycan. "In a sec."

She tsks at me. "Aren't you cold?"

I'm freezing. "Nope." I fire up the gas, boil the water, and make the soup. When I turn back to Holly, she's huddled in a ball with her legs pulled up in front of her and her back resting against the wall, a faded grey blanket draped over her chest and tucked under her armpits. The beach towel is wrapped around her wet hair like a fluffy rainbow-coloured turban. The sight brings a smile to my face and a chuckle escapes me. I hand her the soup. "Drink this. It'll help warm you up."

She takes the billy from my hands and sighs, hugging the small insulated can to her chest. "Don't you want some?"

"Yep. That's why we're sharing," I say as I grab another blanket. "Shove over."

She shuffles sideways, moves her camera bag to the floor, and makes room for me to sit beside her. Wrapping the blanket around myself, I drape my arm across her shoulders and pull her into my side, extending the blanket around her back too. She fidgets a little, although whether it's to get more comfortable or to avoid touching too much of me, I can't tell.

Holly blows on the soup to cool it down then takes a sip. "Mmm... chicken and corn. My favourite."

"I know," I say as she passes me the billy.

Taking a sip from the can, I look around the tiny wooden shed. It's not as nice as some of the boxes in the row, but at least it's clean. The floors are swept, the cobwebs minimal. The daybed and a few collapsible chairs are the only furniture to be found, all of them old and in keeping with the Victorian heritage of the place. A derelict-looking crab pot and a couple of timber oars are tucked up in the rafters, although whether they're for practical use or simple ambiance is anyone's guess.

Listening to the cadence of the rain as it steadily pelts the tin roof, I wonder again about the bloke who owns it. Holly's client, the mysterious Mal. He'd have to be rich. Only locals who live in the exclusive Bayside area are allowed to own one of these things, and the last time one of them went to auction, it sold for more than a quarter of a million dollars.

Not bad for a timber shack that's smaller than the shed I use to store my lawnmower.

And if Holly's dating someone like that, what chance do I have? A fireman who's neck-deep in debt and lives on a diet of two-minute noodles, Cup-a-Soup, and beans on toast just to make ends meet. Okay, so I might be *slightly* exaggerating—my mortgage payments aren't that steep—but shit.

I can't compete with a millionaire.

Not quite managing to keep the bitterness from my

tone, I ask her, "So, how long have you been dating this guy?"

She shivers beside me. "What guy?"

I pull her closer and rub my hand up and down her back, the action perhaps more vigorous than it needs to be. "The guy who owns this little love shack."

There's a frown in her voice when she replies, "I'm not dating Mal."

"Sleeping with him, then. Whatever." I shrug. "How long?"

She shoves at me and I loosen my grip. "Ew. I'm not sleeping with him either. What is with you?"

"Nothing is with me. I'm just curious, that's all." But something eases inside me, and the coil of tension loosens around my heart.

She looks up at me, studying me with a shrewd eye before her sweet lips curve in a wicked grin. "Chris?" She draws out the sound of my name, teasing me with her sensual voice.

I meet her stare with a look of challenge. "What?"

Bumping her shoulder against mine, she says, "Are you jealous?"

I snort. "Of what? You said you're not sleeping with him. And even if you were, what does it matter? I'm too young for you anyway, right?"

As soon as the words leave my mouth, I wish I could take them back. Holly sighs and inches away from me, her grin dissolving into a faint frown that tugs at the corners of her mouth and furrows her brow.

I am such an idiot.

Silence fills the air between us, cautious and awkward. I hate it. I hate that I made her smile disappear, hate that I'm behaving like a total dick.

She deserves better.

The sound of the storm, of the rain pinging off the roof and the wind rattling the doors seems to amplify and fill the void between us, and my mind does what it always does when I fuck up—it overanalyses every detail of the situation until I think I'm going crazy.

Wordlessly, we pass the soup back and forth until there's none left, my brain churning over every little detail until it hits on the one it's searching for.

And the bottom falls out of my gut.

"Let me take that," I say quietly, and I hold out my hand for the empty billy. Holly's hand brushes mine as she passes me the can, a spark of sensation making me shiver. I look at her. She's staring straight ahead at some point on the wall opposite us, staunchly ignoring me. My heart clenches and I swallow hard. "I'm sorry I snapped at you, Hols."

Her voice is so quiet I almost don't hear her over the sound of the storm. "It's okay."

"No, it's not. I shouldn't be taking out my frustrations on you."

"What do you mean?"

I clench my jaw—tight. I don't want her to see how much this is killing me. "When I saw you lying face down in the sand, for a split second I thought—"

She tugs the blanket up to her chin. "You thought I was dead."

My hands fist in the blanket but I resist the urge to pull her closer, giving her space, fearful that if I touch her right now, I'll crush her to me and never let her go.

"I could see the storm was worsening, could see the lightning coming closer, and instead of dragging your stubborn arse inside, I left you to fend for yourself while I fetched my surfboard. You almost died because I prioritised my fucking *surfboard* over you. How could I ever face your parents again, Mike again, knowing I left you alone, that I didn't protect you?"

Turning to face me, she stares me down. She looks mad, and I half expect her to waggle a finger in my face. "If you'd tried to drag me inside, you would've had a fight on your hands every step of the way. I know you're used to rescuing people, but I'm not some delicate little flower, Christopher. I don't need protecting."

"But—"

"No. It's not your fault I did something stupid. That rests on *my* shoulders, not yours. You're allowed to be mad at me, Chris. Hell, I'm mad at me," she said, then added a mumbled, "And not just about today."

Okay. I'm confused. "What do you mean?"

Taking a deep breath and looking up at me from under her lashes, she says, "Do you remember the morning after Mikey's twenty-first birthday bash? You'd promised your mum you'd take her to church, and you were having a shower before you left to pick her up."

I cough a disbelieving laugh and run a hand through my damp hair, the memory not *uncomfortable* exactly, but also not something I thought we'd be sitting around discussing six years later. *Where is she going with this?* "Ah, yeah, I remember. You walked in on me in the shower and caught me... ah... you know."

One corner of her mouth twitches up. "Wanking?"

I didn't think I still owned the ability to blush, not after some of the weird shit I've seen on the job, but bloody hell. Holly always did know which buttons to push. "You thought I was Mike and just barged in like you owned the place."

She ducks her head, then peeks up at me. "Yeah, about that.... I knew you weren't Mike."

My brow shoots up and my eyes widen as I turn to stare at her. "Say what now?"

"I knew it was you. I wanted to... hell, I don't know what I wanted." She shakes her head, her turban tumbling down. She pulls the towel from her hair and drops it on the floor. "I was so confused."

Annnd I'm annoyed again. "You weren't confused the night before when I told you how I felt about you. I remember you being *very* clear about that at the time."

Holly stiffens and lifts her chin. Her words are stilted. "You were twenty-one years old."

"And you were thirty-one years old," I argue, my voice growing louder. "So what?"

Matching my volume, her words are like daggers, slicing at old wounds I thought had healed. "So whether you like it or not, ten years is a big difference. You hadn't dated much and—"

"That's bullshit," I snap, turning on the bed so we're face-to-face. "I dated other women, Hols."

"Not enough!"

Grabbing her arms, I pull her so close our noses almost touch. Dropping my voice to a low rumble, my words are steadfast and sure. "Enough to know I was never going to feel with them what I feel when I'm with you. I know you're never going to love me, Holly, but I will *never* stop loving you."

My chest heaves, every breath shuddering in and out of me, and each one feels like my last. Her tongue flicks over her lips and I want to taste it. I want to suck on it, wrestle with it, feel it licking my cock before her mouth envelops my balls. I want to close that minuscule distance still separating us and claim her as mine, wrap my arms around her and love her with every inch of my being.

Every rock solid inch.

She takes a breath and it whispers over my lips as she exhales. She's calmer now, her voice soft again. "Yeah, well, you're wrong."

And here it comes.

The final blow.

Same as last time.

You're too young, Chris. You'll get over it, Chris.

But then she says something that completely knocks me on my arse. "Because I love you too, you arsehole."

"What did you say?" I pull back so I can see her whole face, watch for the lie.

Looking away as though embarrassed, she mutters, "I called you an arsehole."

My lips twitch. "Before that."

"I said"—her voice drops to a whisper as she peeks up at me again—"I love you too."

I'm dumbfounded. Frozen. I probably look like a stunned mullet with my mouth hanging open and no words coming out, but I don't care because under my skin is a whole other world of sensation. My heart is beating like a wild thing, pumping like crazy, forcing my blood to race through my body and igniting every nerve on fire. A cacophony of sound explodes in my head as every fantasy I've ever held about this woman crashes into the reality of this moment, here and now.

"Say something," she whispers. Hearing the hitch in her voice, I realise I'm still impersonating a dead fish, staring silently as this inferno rages inside me.

Puffing out a breath of shock, I shove my hand through my hair. "Well... fuck me."

A lift of her shoulder is the only warning I get before she shoves my bewildered arse back on the bed. "Okay."

Laughter escapes me. "Hols, that's not what I—" My words die on my tongue, crushed under the weight of my moans as Holly straddles my body and rubs herself along my rock-hard cock, the heat of her pussy burning through the thin barrier of my shorts. Anchoring my hands on her hips, I say, "You know what? I'm just going to—"

"Shut up, Christopher."

My heart is thumping in an uncontrollable rhythm. "Okay."

Grabbing the bottom of her shirt, she pulls it over her head and tosses it on the floor. Her big, soft breasts sit heavily against her chest, her dark pink nipples puckered into hard little buds. My hands itch to touch them, to finally feel their weight in my palms, to pluck those sweet rosebuds between my fingers until she cries out her pleasure. She leans over me, and I swallow hard, lick my lips, and watch with rapt attention as her breasts swing ever closer to my mouth. My hands tighten on her hips.

"I want you, Chris. I wanted you then and I want you now, and I'm sorry I hurt you. I was afraid of the way I felt. Confused. I was engaged to someone else, but I had all these feelings for you too and I didn't know what to do with them, so I just shoved them down and prayed they'd go away."

"Did they?" I ask, hissing out a breath as she slides back down my cock. "Go away?"

She smiles, shy and sweet. "No. They never did."

Reaching up, I slide my hands through her hair and guide her mouth to mine. I've waited so long to feel her soft lips, taste her sweet breath. Holding her steady, a hair's breadth away, I ask, "Are you sure you want to do this?"

"Very sure. But I should tell you, I haven't been with a man since I got divorced."

Only eighteen months?

My lips twitch into a lopsided smile and I shrug. "That's okay. I haven't been with a woman since you got married."

Just as her eyes widen, I close the distance between us and press my lips to hers. Soft and warm and responsive, she slides her tongue along the seam of my mouth, and I open up and let her in. A moan escapes me as I taste Holly for the first time, as the heat of her tongue lashes against mine.

Sliding my hands down her back, I savour the feel of her smooth skin, feeling the warmth of her body pressed against mine. I rip the blankets away, discarding them on the floor. We don't need them anymore, not now we have a better way of warming each other up.

Holly rocks her hips and grinds her pussy against my cock, but I can't *feel* her. Not the way I want. My board-shorts are in the way. I'm about to tell her to stop so I can take them off when she shimmies backwards, taking my boardies with her. My cock springs free, bouncing against my stomach.

Her tongue flicks out and moistens her lips as she stares at me, at my dick, with a look of hunger and need. "Sit on the edge of the bed." I do as requested and swing my legs over the edge so I'm sitting up again. Holly gathers the discarded blankets under her and kneels on the floor, pushes my legs apart, and smiles up at me. "I've always wanted to do this for you," she says and reaches up to kiss me again. "Relax."

Relax?

The woman of my dreams is on her knees between my

legs, staring at my dick like it's an all-you-can-eat buffet, and she wants me to relax?

Yeah, that is so not gunna happen.

Placing a hand on my chest, she gently pushes me backwards until I'm leaning against the wall of the box, the painted timber smooth and cool against my back. Gaze fixed firmly on mine, she wraps one hand around my cock, leans forwards, and licks in one long, slow stroke from base to tip.

My mouth falls open and a voice not quite my own emits a low, guttural growl. "Holy fuck."

I wasn't joking when I told her I hadn't had a woman in almost five years. I mean, sure, I've been on dates. I've made out with other women—kissing, heavy petting, that sort of thing. But that's as far as it ever went. Maybe it's because I was raised by a single mum, or maybe it's just my own moral code, but I've never slept with a woman on the first date.

And since my job involves shift work and revolves around unpredictable circumstances like idiots smoking in bed and accidentally burning their houses down, second dates are pretty much non-existent.

Holly licks me again, and again and again, but when she opens her mouth and sinks down over the head of my shaft, I lose my fucking mind. I'd forgotten how good it feels to be enveloped in the warmth of something more appealing than my own hand. She works my cock with an expert touch, knows just how hard to suck, where to lick, when to bite.

And then she squeezes my balls.

Fuck yeah!

I slide my hand through her hair, guiding her as she pumps her mouth up and down my cock, making my sensitive flesh wet. Then she sits back on her heels and grins up at me.

"Ready?"

I narrow my eyes. "For what?"

"This."

Cupping her breasts, she squeezes them around my shaft then bounces up and down, fucking me with her tits. The pressure, the heat, the slick slide of her soft flesh against my dick feels amazing. Just when I thought it couldn't get any better, she flicks her tongue out and laps at the tip of my cock every time it pokes its head out from between her Double-D's.

Never in my wildest fantasies—and there've been a lot—did I ever imagine she could look so dirty and so sexy at the same time. Pre-come coats the tip of my shaft, and I groan as she greedily laps it up.

Feels. So. Good!

Too good.

"Hols, baby, you keep that up and I—oh *fuck*, I'm gunna come."

No sooner do the words leave my lips than my cock is being swallowed down her throat. She sucks me down and works my flesh, flicks her tongue, grabs my balls, stares at me with those gorgeous blue eyes of hers and watches as I come undone in her hands and in her mouth. My hips jerk and I cry out, my orgasm blinding me to everything but the woman wringing this pleasure from my body like the goddess she is.

Slumping back, panting and satiated, my body shakes, shivers, but not from the cold. I've never felt so hot in all my life. And I'm a fucking firefighter.

Holly crawls into my lap, straddling my thighs once more. Her pussy feels swollen and wet where she pushes against me. "I want to fuck," she says, then nibbles a path around the shell of my ear and across my collarbone.

"You need to give me time to recover, baby."

She pouts at me and I can't help but grin.

"How much time?"

"Long enough for me to return the favour, I'd reckon."

She laughs as I tumble her back onto the daybed, her voice clear and sweet, totally at odds with the naughty seductress who just blew my mind.

Holding myself over her, I lower my head and suck her nipple into my mouth, nip it with my teeth. Back arching, she moans and thrusts her breasts upwards, eager for my attention. Sliding my hand between her legs, I slip one finger deep inside her, feel how wet she is, how soft and ready to be filled.

Dragging my fingers from her pussy and up over her belly, I trace them around her nipple, using her own moisture to draw on her supple flesh before licking it away, sucking it clean.

"More."

Reaching between her legs again, I sink two fingers inside her. "Greedy girl."

I continue sucking her nipples, alternating from one to the other as I piston my fingers in and out of her pussy. My hand is soaked. My cock twitches as I kiss a path heading down, her hands tangling in my hair, encouraging my journey south.

When I reach the junction between her thighs, I take my time to savour the view, watching in awe as her cunt hungrily sucks my fingers back inside every time I withdraw them. Her thighs are coated in juice, slick and shiny. Leaning down, I run my tongue along her sensitive flesh and smile as she quivers at my touch.

"Chris. Please."

Two little words.

That's all it takes to bend me to her will.

Dipping my head between her legs, I go straight for the kill, sucking and licking her perfect little clit, eating her pussy like a man possessed. She tastes amazing, sweet and warm. She feels fantastic, soft and hot. Her body undulates beneath me, her breaths little more than ragged gasps for air.

She's close. So close.

Her fingernails score my scalp as she holds me where she wants me, until she's sucking great gulps of air, fucking my face and screaming my name, the sound so loud she drowns out the storm still raging around us.

"Holy shit." She pants the words with a quiet laugh, and I rest my chin on her mound.

"Still want that fuck?"

Lifting her head to look down at me, a grin splitting her face from ear to ear, she bites her lip and nods. "Please tell me you have protection."

"I'm a fireman," I say as I rip open the side pocket on my bag and pull out a box of condoms. "I'm prepared for any emergency." And just because sleeping with Holly was always going to be a long shot, doesn't mean I wasn't hopeful enough to grab a pack on my way here.

Sitting beside her, my cock juts up from between my legs, eager and proud. Holly takes the box of condoms from me, slips one out, and rolls it over my hard length. I suck in a breath at the gentle torture.

"Lie down," she says, pressing me back on the mattress as she straddles my hips once more. Rocking her body against mine, she positions herself above me and wastes no time sliding slowly down my cock, enveloping me in her heat.

"Holly." I send up her name like a prayer, whispered in the darkness to give me strength.

Locking my hands around her hips, I hold on for the ride, thrusting up to meet her as she grinds herself down, my cock hitting her deep inside and making her moan. Her hair is a tangled mess, but it frames her face so beautifully. Her body is flushed a pretty pink, and sweat beads between her heavy breasts.

She's everything I've ever wanted, everything I'll ever need, and suddenly my hands are bunching her hair at her nape, forcing her mouth to meet mine. Our tongues and teeth wage war, licking, thrusting, tasting, biting. I snake one arm around her middle and lock her against me, revelling in the feel of her lushness squashed against my hard chest. Hips thrusting, flesh slapping, her pussy is like a vice around my cock, tight and wet and so fucking hot.

Sweat drips from my brow and I grit my teeth as that familiar feeling of ecstasy builds inside me. Sliding my hands down her back, I cup her arse and move her faster, fucking us both into oblivion.

Holly comes first, screaming my name and a string of profanities at the top of her lungs. I follow fast on her heels with a shout of my own and a vow of whatever the fuck the opposite of chastity is, because there is no way in hell I'm never doing this again.

Afterwards, we both lay there, dragging in breath after breath, waiting for our heart rates to calm, then I shift her to my side and dispose of the condom.

When I crawl into bed beside her, Holly snuggles against my chest and drapes her leg over mine. The feel of her soft pussy pressed against my muscled thigh makes my cock twitch with renewed life, but I force the sensation back and drag the blanket over us, focus on holding Holly, on keeping her warm and safe.

"So what happens now?" she says quietly, her breath

tickling my skin.

"We wait for the storm to pass, go home, get Chinese from that place you like, and have more sex."

She pokes me in the ribs. "That's not what I meant and you know it."

Tucking an arm under my head, I smile up at the rafters. "I know. But in all honesty, Hols, I don't care what happens next. The world could fall down around us and I wouldn't care, as long as we're together."

She stares at me with narrowed eyes for a moment, then leans up to kiss me. "Okay, fine. But I get to tell Mikey." She chuckles maniacally. "I can't wait to see the look on his face. And I want Thai food, not Chinese."

I nod with a chuckle of my own, let loose some of the the happiness expanding inside me. "Thai it is."

Looking around the bathing box, I spy the Santa hat and the inflatable kangaroos and the bright red boardshorts covered in surfing koalas, and I know there's no other woman in the world I would've done this for.

Holly has owned my heart for as long as I can remember, and now she owns my arse. But when she slides her hand across my belly, tucks herself close to my side, and murmurs, "I love you, babe," I'm pretty sure I own hers too.

Her perfect, naughty, sexy arse.

And what more could a man want for Christmas?

CARVED IN STONE

For Screech and Boo, who gave me the idea in the first place.

Chapter One

A *rnaath*

ALL DAY I've watched Chloe trudge boxes from the truck to the house, moving her entire life one cubic foot at a time.

I don't know how many years I've waited for her to return home. How long has it been since she discovered her imaginary friend wasn't imaginary, since she blabbed about it to her parents, who promptly shipped her off to boarding school, then sold the house and moved far, far away?

Admittedly, the way Chloe found out I was real could have gone better. I hadn't meant to startle her, and I certainly hadn't meant for her to fall off the damn roof, but she'd tried to kiss me! And call me old-fashioned, but a girl's first kiss should be with a boy her own age, not an ancient lump of rock like me.

Although, as I watch the seductive sway of her hips as she carries a chair up the front steps and into the house, I know I wouldn't mind if she kissed me now. Little Chloe isn't so little anymore. Only a full-grown woman walks with that much swagger, and I wonder with a smile if she's still as gloriously weird as she was as a child.

You see, that's how Chloe and I became friends all those years ago. Imaginary friends, but still. Children her own age thought her peculiar.

I could see why they'd think that. Collecting animal skulls and sleeping with jars full of spiders beside the bed is not exactly usual behaviour for a child, especially a young lady, but Chloe never cared what anyone else thought and simply did it anyway. Just like she defied her parents and climbed up to the roof at every available chance to sit at my side and chatter away about the people buried in the graveyard behind her house, to wonder at the lives they must have led.

Not that she knew I was listening. Not really.

She was a special child—one of the last of her kind, if I had to guess—for she carries the blood of the masters.

The stone masons who created me and my kind.

Some people call us gargoyles, but a *gargoyle* is nothing more than a glorified drainpipe. They are crudely shaped, slack-jawed layabouts, content in their demeaning existence. They are repulsive, and I am most definitely *not* that. Although I'd be lying if I said a number of my brethren didn't make good use of their gaping maws from time to time, but I digress.

I, Arnaath, am a *grotesque*, a guardian who protects the people and wards off evil.

It's an unusual name, I grant you, for someone as spectacular as myself, and not the name given to my kind originally. When we were created, when the masters carved us from the purest marble and gave us the faces of fallen angels with bodies to match, we were known as something quite different.

Canterbury's Wolves.

It is universally acknowledged that even in the toughest of times, prostitutes make money, and in the twelfth century, the churches and the bishops knew a good thing when they saw it and taxed said prostitutes, taking a little— or a large—piece of the pie for themselves.

But here's the thing: humans in the Middle Ages were not the cleanest of individuals, and if the missus didn't kill you for visiting the stews, the syphilis would, and the church took their cut either way.

The archbishop of Canterbury was a clever man, and using his knowledge of courtier life and who was—or was *not*—sleeping with whom, he had the idea to keep the money coming in by tapping into a frequently overlooked and underutilised source of capital.

High-born women.

After all, what's good for the gander is good for the goose. But, ever aware of the scandal that would arise if the fairer half of his flock suddenly contracted an STD, or worse, fell pregnant while their husbands were otherwise occupied with one crusade or another, he gathered the best sculptors money could buy and gave them a task.

Me and my stony brethren.

But it didn't matter how exquisitely carved we were, every detail of our marble bodies painstaking and precise, we were still lifeless lumps of rock. No better than statues. But it turns out all those secret societies the conspiracy nuts are always banging on about were actually a thing way back when, and not only were the masters handy with a chisel, but some of them knew their way around the art of anthropomorphism too.

One by one they breathed life into us, gave us emotions and thoughts and a sense of touch, and before we even knew what we were, we were being instructed in the finer points of pleasuring a woman for coin.

Yes. That's right. I was a medieval man of the night.

A lady knew when she entered our den that she had no chance of contracting the pox or falling with child. Safe from the fragility of male egos and assured a night of pleasure, she was the most important woman in the world, free to sin, to indulge her baser desires, even if only for an hour or two, depending on the size of her purse. And on those rare occasions when women were scarce, well, that's where the gargoyles and their gaping mouths come into play.

And now you're probably scratching your pretty little heads wondering how I went from prostitute to pigeon post.

Well, the way we came by our name of *grotesque* was violent and painful and cruel beyond measure—there's a reason most of my brethren are as anatomically correct as a Ken doll, and it has nothing to do with the ravages of time. No, as educated as we were in the ways of women and their pleasure, we were innocent of the ways of men and their petty jealousies.

They attacked us.

Resentful husbands and outraged fathers smashed and hacked and shattered us. Broke horns. Ripped off wings. Gouged out eyes and cut off cocks. And when they'd finished, leaving us in various states of rubble, they hunted down and murdered our masters, ensuring we remained broken and ugly—*grotesque*. Ensuring their women would never seek comfort in our arms again.

But I was one of the lucky ones.

My creator survived and managed to restore me to my

former glory. Well, mostly. Definitely all the parts that matter.

And upon inspecting the carnage and seeing what had become of those who could not be made whole again, the archbishop offered us a different life from the one we'd known, and like so many eunuchs before them, my brothers resigned themselves to a life of duty within the church. They took to the rooves, to the steeples and belfries, so they could watch over their lovers, protect them from afar.

And perhaps take a little pleasure in haunting their attackers, reminding them they would never satisfy their women as well as an ugly and broken-down lump of rock. And even though my creator had left me mostly whole and hearty, I joined my brethren at their post and settled into the new life the archbishop had granted us.

But time really is the enemy of the immortal. Endless, ceaseless, mind-numbing time. Watching each excruciating second slip into the next and the next and so on and so forth....

God, I was bored.

I went from pleasuring women every night, hearing them sigh and moan and cry out their ecstasy, knowing I had done my job well and would be rewarded with another willing female the next night and the next, to being the medieval equivalent of a hood ornament for the archbishop's pimp-mobile.

I lasted less than a year before I decided the church was not for me and struck out on my own.

Now, I know you're wondering what the fuck this has to do with anything and how the hell I ended up on the roof of a reclaimed country church in the middle of buttfuck nowhere, and I'm getting to that.

It turned out the world wasn't ready for anthropomorphic sculptures who loved to fuck, and not long after I liberated myself from the cathedral in Canterbury, I went back into hiding, tucking myself up in the back of a tithe barn where I figured the local priest wouldn't bother to look for me. And while in hiding, I kinda, maybe fell asleep for a century or two.

Or seven.

You know how it is when you wake up after a really weird dream and it takes you a moment to get your bearings and realise you're still in bed? Well, don't fall asleep for seven hundred-plus years and expect to wake up where you fell asleep.

No, I woke up just as I was being offloaded from a ship. And when the crate they'd boxed me in was opened, a man who looked vaguely like my creator told me my whoring days were done, then brought me to this church-come-quirky-country-cottage I now sit upon and told me to behave myself.

"Arnaath?"

Shit. I got so lost in my musings I didn't hear Chloe climb up to the roof. I dare not move. Not yet. If I had a heart, it would be beating its way out of my chest right about now. If I had breath, it would be stuttering in and out of my lungs.

I'm nervous, though I'm not sure how I know that. I don't think I've ever been nervous before.

"Arnaath, I know you can hear me," she says, her words hesitant, like she doesn't fully believe what she's saying.

Her voice is richer than the last time I heard it. Fuller, more grown-up. More sensual. It makes me shiver, and my cock starts to rise. The tentative touch of her hand sliding along the edge of my wing, the warmth of her soft skin, makes me smile.

I forget to be nervous. "You're not allowed up here, little mason," I say. "What if you fall off the roof again?"

Slowly I turn to look at her. I can't not look at her. I've watched her all day, wanted to reach out and touch her all day.

Standing with her arms akimbo and one brow cocked, she says, "I didn't fall. You pushed me."

If it wasn't for the cheeky glint in her eyes or the lifting of one corner of her mouth, I'd be insulted. "I didn't push you, wench," I tell her, folding my arms across my chest. "You surprised me."

"Surprised you." She scoffs. "I kissed you."

"You tried."

"You saying there was something wrong with my kiss?"

"Since you think I pushed you off the roof afterwards, you tell me."

For a brief moment, Chloe's expression resembles that of a gasping fish. Then she bursts out laughing and shakes her head. "I knew you were real. I knew I wasn't crazy. And my father knew, too, didn't he? Or he wouldn't have made us move house when I'd insisted you'd saved me. I can't believe he actually tried the old 'you were dreaming' trick." She rolls her eyes. "As if that would ever work."

Grinning at her indignation, I nod, confirming her suspicion. "Yes, your father knew," I say. "And he was none too happy with me after that little incident."

Her eyes widen. "He was unhappy you saved me?"

"He was unhappy that my allure caused his only child to put herself in harm's way. And thankfully *all* he did was move you away from me. Especially after he threatened to take a hammer and chisel to my cock and balls." I can't quite suppress the shudder that run along my spine and flutters my wings. "Forcing me back into endless slumber was definitely the lesser of two evils."

Her brow pulls down, and I have the urge to reach out and smooth it away. Or maybe any excuse to touch her will do. "What do you mean by 'endless slumber'?"

I yawn and stretch, the vestiges of my latest sleep still dissipating. "As I discovered many moons ago, when I am apart from my creator's bloodline for too long, I fall into a deep sleep. I become the statue you know and adore. A failsafe, so your father told me, to prevent me and my brothers from running amok. So as it was with your father when he first shipped me here from merry ol' England, being near to you has awoken me again."

Chloe looks unimpressed by this knowledge and folds her arms across her ample bosom, drawing my gaze to follow the contours of all that softness. My cock stiffens against my thigh, and I lick my lips.

"That's the excuse you're going with? Really? You didn't once offer to help me unload the truck because you were what? Defrosting?" she says, but again there is a teasing lilt under the surface of her words.

So I tease back. "You want me to pitch you off the roof again?"

She looks pointedly at her full, lush figure, then back at me, the challenge clear in her dark blue eyes. "I'd like to see you try."

Chapter Two

C*hloe*

ARNAATH'S SMILE is slow and disarming. My old friend is big and built for strength, and his reflexes haven't dulled with age. In the blink of an eye, he hauls me against his naked chest and squeezes the soft globes of my arse.

When my feet leave the ground, my stomach drops and I wrap my arms around his head, inadvertently burying his face in my cleavage. "Don't you dare!" I say. Well, squeal is a more apt description. The unnaturally high pitch of my voice makes me wince, but after my fall all those years ago, I no longer do so well with heights. And Arnaath isn't just big, he's tall too. Close to seven feet.

"Or what?" Arnaath's deep, accented voice is muffled by my flesh, and it's a good thing he doesn't need to breathe. At least, I really hope he doesn't need to breathe, because I have no intention of letting go until my feet are on solid ground again.

"Or I'll... um...." I'm shaking, my bravado banished in the face of my greatest fear. "Please put me down."

But even after I feel the roof beneath my feet, I find I am sufficiently freaked out, to the point that I can't seem to loosen my grip on Arnaath's head, and it's only when he pries me off him that I'm able to take a step back.

And he immediately grabs me again. "Careful!"

Glancing over my shoulder, I realise I was about to back into the parapet that edges the flat portion of the roof. It's not particularly tall and is easy to trip over.

Ask me how I know.

A whimper escapes me, and I find myself wrapped not only in Arnaath's arms but his wings too, warm and secure. Safe. "I've got you, little mason. I won't let you fall again."

His body is so warm, his skin so soft. But how? He's made of stone. How the hell is any of this possible?

Maybe I really am crazy. Maybe this is all just a figment of my imagination and I'm actually just a lunatic hugging an inanimate sculpture on the roof of my childhood home. But as he hugs me tighter and my breasts and belly squash against the press of his hard, muscular chest, I figure as delusions go this ain't so bad.

Especially when I feel what I'm hoping is his cock dig into my thigh.

"You're shaking like a leaf," he murmurs by my ear, and again I hear a soft burr in his tone. It sounds odd, like the way he speaks, a mishmash of old and new.

"Of course I'm shaking. We're two storeys up and *way* outside my comfort zone."

Arnaath presses a kiss to the top of my head. "Then may I suggest we get down from here?"

I nod, grateful—until he scoops me up and takes a running leap at the edge of the roof.

Burying my head in the crook of his neck, I stifle my scream, refusing to watch as we plunge downwards. But instead of the thud of us crashing into the ground, the air fills with the sound of Arnaath's strong wings flaring wide and his devious laughter. The sensation of falling makes my stomach flip like it does on a rollercoaster, but the sound of Arnaath's joy washes away my fear.

How long has it been since he moved this freely? Since he talked to someone? Since he soared through the air? How long has it been since my family abandoned him?

How long have I been trying to get back to him?

A moment later he puts me down, my feet sinking into the tangle of ivy that covers the yard and threatens to envelope the rear of the house.

"Sorry, little mason," he says, grinning, his wings settling against his back as he strokes my jaw with the blade of his finger. "I couldn't resist."

I slap my hands against his shoulder and give him a shove, not that it does anything other than make him laugh again. "Arsehole." But the word lacks heat as my own laughter bubbles out of me. "Come on, then," I say, opening the back door to the cottage. "It's getting cold out here."

My house is an odd-looking thing. Originally built as a church over a hundred years ago and designed to look like a small castle, it was an interesting place to grow up, what with the stained-glass windows and the backyard full of dead people and all.

I loved it!

And yeah, before you run away thinking, "Weird-O!" let me just say that being normal isn't something I've often been accused of.

I know I'm strange, okay?

I am *very* aware of that fact.

I was reminded of it every other day of my life growing up until finally, one day, I simply accepted that I was "that" girl. I was the weird girl no one wanted to sit next to in class, who grew up to become the weird chick who couldn't get a date, who went on to take over the family masonry business and bought back my childhood home, the one that came with its very own graveyard.

And a large marble statue of a nearly naked demon on the roof.

Not that I have to worry about anyone seeing me. The house sits on the outskirts of town, way back from the edge of a lonely pockmarked road. A sad ramshackle excuse of a building hidden behind an unruly thicket of hazelnuts and blackberry brambles, its exterior leaves much to be desired.

In the twenty years since I fell off the roof, the old girl has had four owners. Each of them well-intentioned and enthusiastic and chock-a-block full of the overconfidence that can only be garnered by watching too many home renovation shows on "reality" TV.

Of course, when they found out exactly how much it would cost to renovate the quaint stone castle in the middle of bloody Nowheresville, they put it back on the market quicker than you can say "money pit". The upshot being that every time it went back on the market, the value dropped just a little closer to what I could afford.

So here I am, the proud owner of a DIYer's wet dream, following the walking embodiment of another sort of wet dream as we enter my kitchen.

It's dark in the house, and cold. I haven't had the electricity turned on yet, but I did put a box of candles on the kitchen table, so we'll have some light at least. Squeezing past Arnaath, I find what I'm looking for and light just enough candles to give the room a soft glow.

Then my guest takes one of those lit candles and my box of matches and moves through to the living room.

I follow behind him, my eyes narrowed in curiosity. Why would a creature like him need light to see? "So, no supernatural night vision, then?"

He rests the candle on the mantel, then kneels down to set a fire in the hearth. "I'm made of marble, not cats," he says, but even when teasing, the sound of his voice draws me closer, like an invisible thread weaving around us, slowly tightening, binding us together. I wonder if his voice was designed to do that. To be pleasing, to draw women to him. To tempt and ensnare them.

To seduce them.

It was only a year ago that my mother finally told me what Arnaath truly was and where he had come from. My father had confessed to her before he'd died of silicosis—Stonemason's Disease—and she'd thought it beyond time I knew the truth about my imaginary friend.

The story she'd told me had been unreal. I mean, Arnaath? A medieval gargoyle prostitute? Really? And yes, I know he's not technically a gargoyle, but holy shit!

Arnaath was a gigolo.

A male escort.

A... medieval sex doll!

No wonder he looks so damn enticing, but I guess he wouldn't have made the bishop much money if he didn't look the part.

It also makes sense that he was my first crush. No normal boys for this weirdo. Nope. Give me a stony-faced, rock-hard bodied, winged beast of a man any day.

I didn't stand a chance against my lithographic lothario.

As the fire crackles to life, it casts its yellow light into the room and splashes across Arnaath's alabaster skin, highlighting marble so smooth and pale it's almost ethereal. I want to reach out and touch him. I want to drag my fingertips over every slab of muscle, through every strand of hair.

I want to know what makes him... *him*.

And I want to know how he lost one horn, and why he has one eye made of amethyst, and why he's missing two toes off his left foot.

As he feeds more wood to the fire, he catches me watching him and smiles again, only this time the smile is seductive. His eyes too, letting his eyelids fall to half mast as he returns my stare. The look is potent, hypnotic, and I'm finding it hard to look away.

I move closer. "My mother told me about you," I say, then tell him everything she told me, everything my father had told her. "Did she leave anything out?"

Pushing to his feet, he dusts his hands off on the simple cloth habit wrapped around his waist, and I watch even that mundane action with a curiosity I can't hide. Not from him. Then he holds out his hands to the fire as though warming them. It's such a human thing to do, but Arnaath isn't human.

"She got the gist of it correct. I am stone brought to life, and I was, for all intents and purposes, a prostitute." He turns that intense gaze on me again, but any hint of his smile has vanished. "Does that bother you?"

I shake my head. "No. Not in the slightest." His past is his own and I'm not one to judge.

He nods once as if to signal the end of that portion of our Q&A session and turns to face me fully, his eyes narrowed, his head tilted to one side in the perfect expression of curiosity. "Why was your mother the one to tell you about me? Where is your father?"

I swallow down the lump in my throat and grit my teeth to keep my emotions from overwhelming me. "He passed away. A year ago." I roll my shoulders to ease the tightness there.

It's still too soon.

But in an instant, I'm in Arnaath's arms again, and he settles my head against his chest, tucking me under his chin. "I am sorry, little mason. Your father was a good man. A sizeable pain in my arse, but a good man nonetheless. He saved me from an eternity of boredom. Not that I'd have been awake to notice. If he hadn't found me and brought me here, I'd have probably ended up decorating some rich idiot's garden." He stiffened. "Or worse, on an episode of *Antiques Roadshow*."

My sadness steps back to give my shock room to move. I lean back and stare up at him, frowning. "How do you know about *Antiques Roadshow*?"

He smiles affectionately. "Your father used to invite me inside sometimes, when you and your mother were out. He'd let me watch television and teach me about this modern world I'd woken up in. Then threaten my manhood if I so much as blinked in front of you."

Watching TV certainly answers my question about the odd way he speaks, but still I shake my head, both baffled and annoyed at my dad for his pig-headed ways. "Why didn't he just tell us about you? Why all the secrecy?"

Arnaath cups my face and his smile takes on that seductive tilt again. "I do not know. And I do not care. It is in the past, little mason. Where it belongs."

"But—"

"But nothing," he says, leaning down, bringing his lips

so close to my own I can feel the heat of him. "You are cold, and it's beyond time I warmed you up."

My tongue darts out to lick my lips. "Warm me up?" There are so many naughty images racing through my head right now, it's hard to focus.

"You're shivering. You have been since we were on the roof."

"Maybe I'm just excited to see you again," I tell him without a single scrap of shame.

"Or maybe you need to take off your inadequate clothing and allow me to care for you," he says, a stern tone strengthening his words and making them sound very reasonable.

But they're anything but reasonable, and I shoot him my best raised eyebrow look of dubiousness. "I have to get naked for you to care for me?"

His sudden grin highlights the squareness of his jaw, and I almost swoon in the face of so much hotness. "No," he says with a wink. "But being naked will make it a lot more fun."

His words carry a hint of a dare, and his sexy grin is just flat out taunting me. And while I was never one to bow to peer pressure—weird girl with zero friends, remember?—I never shied away from a challenge either.

And Arnaath is definitely challenging me.

Chapter Three

 *rnaath*

CHLOE NARROWS her eyes at my reasoning, but just when I think she'll turn tail and run from me, my girl surprises me and demands, "Turn around."

With a languid smile, I do as instructed and face the fireplace, then listen in torturous rapture to the sounds of her undressing, every little movement, every rustle of fabric echoing in my ears until one salacious image after another dances through my mind.

Images of Chloe's soft body, of her hair let loose so it spills across her shoulders and down her long back. Of her strong arms and thick thighs, the generous curve of her hips, the swell of her stomach and plentiful breasts....

My cock hardens with such speed that if I actually had a blood supply, the draining of it from my body to fill my cock would leave me dizzy.

Chloe is my favourite type of woman. Big and bold and spectacularly sexy.

"All right, you can turn around now."

I close my eyes, letting my anticipation linger as I turn to face her. But when I open my eyes, I see more than a naked woman, more than my friend, more than Chloe. I see the life I should have had, the life of a real man. The life I'll never have.

When I look at Chloe, I see the wife I crave, the mother of the children I'll never give her.

The keeper of my heart.

As much as any man ever had one. A heart, that is.

"Say something," she whispers.

But I can't. My voice has deserted me along with my wits.

Only one thought remains.

Mine.

All I can do is reach for the tie at my waist that holds my habit in place and tug it loose, allowing the enchanted stone to pool at my feet like the fabric it was carved to imitate, and let her see my desire for her.

She watches, fascinated, as the cloth falls away, then drags her gaze higher. I know when she reaches my very large, very erect cock because her eyes widen and her cheeks darken with colour. "Oh," she murmurs.

Stepping towards her, I hold out my arms and beckon her to me, pushing away my melancholy. "Time to warm you up," I say with a grin, then pull her into my embrace and move her towards the fireplace, rubbing my hands up and down her back and arms, smoothing the goosebumps from her cool flesh. I flirt with temptation as I brush my fingertips along the sides of her breasts.

"Arnaath," she says quietly, rubbing her cheek against

my chest, "how is this possible? How are *you* possible?" She turns her head to gaze up at me, curiosity and wonder dancing in her eyes. "How is a marble statue warm to the touch when it's been overcast all day? How is your skin soft when you're made from stone? How does your hair move in the breeze? How did the cloth tied around your waist fall to the floor as if it wasn't carved in stone? How is *any* of this possible?"

"It's a kind of magic," I whisper. "But you already know that. You always were a clever girl, little mason. No, I think what you really want to ask me is... why? Why didn't I tell you what I was? Why did I follow your father's orders and pretend to be the statue?" I trace my fingertips along her jaw and tip up her chin. "Why didn't I let you kiss me?"

Her intake of breath is quick and quiet, but enough to make her chest rise and press her breasts firmer against me, and all I want to do is lean down and take one in my mouth. Savour the feel of her on my tongue, pull the scent of her deep inside me.

But I dare not rush her.

It's a lot to take in.

She doesn't quite pout when she says, "I figured that last one was an act of chivalry on your part."

Chivalry.

It was anything but.

It was an act of self-preservation.

But standing here, now, with her wrapped in my arms, feeling her silky skin and soft body pressed against my hard one, I know I should push her away, push her in the direction of a flesh-and-blood man, one who would appreciate her as much as I do. Her endless wit, her tremendous laugh, her determination, and sexy-as-fuck body.

But I can't. I'm a selfish prick. "I want to kiss you,

Chloe. I shouldn't. I shouldn't want you as much as I do. You shouldn't be here, not with me." I lean my forehead against hers and sigh. "You should be with a real man."

Warm fingers slide over my shoulders and brush against my wings, knit behind my neck. She smiles. "You are a real man."

"You know what I mean."

"Yes. And I know what *I* mean," she says, then looks up at me from under long thick eyelashes. "Arnaath, you've always been real to me. Even before I knew you were alive."

And that's when every care and concern and objection I have die a swift death and I can deny her no longer. My mouth crashes against Chloe's, and I give her what she wants.

Take what I want.

She gasps, clearly shocked by the swiftness of my actions, and I take advantage, sweeping my tongue inside her mouth and devouring her.

The sensation is... heady. Wild. Passionate.

And I love that she's right there with me. Love the feel of her arms tightening around my back, her fingernails digging into me, the warmth of her lips, the sweetness of her flavour, the sound of her sultry moans as she rubs her body against mine.

Thank God or the Devil or whoever it was who gave my master the artistry and knowledge to make me what I am. I was designed to pleasure women, to fulfil their every sordid fantasy, but never have I ever felt as powerful as I do right now, knowing Chloe finds pleasure in something as simple as my kisses.

But when she wraps her hand around my rock-hard cock, she completely destroys me.

"Arn," she murmurs as she nibbles her way up the

column of my throat, then latches her teeth around my earlobe. "Fuck me." She strokes my dick with a firm, sure hand. "Please."

Staring down and seeing her undisguised lust screaming back at me, the urge to throw her down to the floor and fuck my way inside her lush body, to feel her thick thighs cradle my muscular ones as I thrust deep, is almost overwhelming. But some small portion of reasoning reminds me of our surroundings.

A near empty house with little to no provisions.

I should carry her to the bedroom, but I'm loath to take her away from the warmth of the fire. And as for throwing her down where we stand, well, apparently some small sliver of chivalry still exists inside of me, because there is no way I'm boning my lover on a cold stone floor after one little kiss.

Even I have better standards than that.

But I can't deny that we need a bed and we need one now, and as luck would have it, there is a solution close at hand.

Chapter Four

C*hloe*

"HOLD THAT THOUGHT," Arnaath murmurs against my lips, then pulls away. Then his lips slam against mine again as if he can't bear to let me go, and my insides melt in happiness.

When he releases me again, he's breathing hard—or at least his body imitates breathing hard—and the corners of his mouth lift in a sinful smile. The type of smile that makes smart women do stupid things.

Like begging giant marble statues to fuck them.

And while I still don't understand the magic that enables him to behave like a "real man", or why my father never told me the truth about all of this, I find I'm beginning to care less and less.

The fact of the matter is Arnaath is real.

And I'm *not* crazy.

Because, yes, actually that has been a small niggling issue at the back of my mind for twenty years. Had I seen what I thought I saw, had Arnaath caught me before I fell to my death, or was I barking mad? Or—as Dad had so unhelp-fully suggested—had I simply fallen asleep and dreamed I was falling, dreamed Arnaath had saved me?

But no. I hadn't. And to be honest, it's nice to finally know the truth. To know I'm normal.

As normal as a weirdo like me can be.

Arn vanishes into another part of the house, and while I wait for him to return from wherever he's disappeared to, I warm myself by the fire. Arnaath was right, I am cold. But I don't have to wait long for him to reappear, and when he does, he's carrying a massive bundle of bed linens, cushions and my purple mink blanket, all of which he dumps on the couch, then gets to work.

I stifle a laugh behind my hand at the view of this tall muscular creature building what essentially looks like a pillow fort on the floor between the fireplace and the couch. "Want some help?"

Instead of replying, he wraps his arms around my thighs and tackles me to the ground, landing me in the middle of his construction with a soft thump. The air rushes out of me, and I'm left gasping as I try to breathe and laugh at the same time and wind up with the hiccups. Because nothing says sexy more than the inability to speak without making strange choking noises. I wish I could just bury my head under the blankets and die of embarrassment.

This reunion is not going how I imagined it would.

Arnaath stares down at me with concern. "Are you well, love?"

A small squeak escapes my lips, an audible testament to my excitement at hearing him call me "love", but I hold my breath and give him a thumbs up. When I'm able to speak again, I say, "I'm fine, really." Then, to cover my unease, I reach for my lover and pull him down on top of me.

I've always been a big girl, but Arnaath doesn't seem to care. When he turned around earlier and saw me naked, when he stood there staring and not saying anything, I'd had a moment of panic. He wouldn't have been the first bloke to tell me he wanted me when my clothes were on only to bolt out the door when my clothes came off.

But he didn't run.

And he didn't make fun of me.

He just took off his own clothes, set his enormous cock free and pulled me into his arms. Arms that held me so securely it felt like no one and nothing could ever hurt me.

Just like that day on the roof.

I'd been trying to get up the nerve to kiss Arnaath for weeks. I was sixteen and knew logically that kissing statues was weird, but I'd also long accepted the fact that I was also weird, which in my twisted teen lizard brain meant kissing a statue was totally normal behaviour. Just another Tuesday.

But then my mum called out to me that dinner was ready, and I knew she'd be angry if she discovered me in the one place I'd been expressly told not to go, and I panicked.

Instead of taking my time and kissing him properly, I rushed it and just kinda slammed my mouth against his. It was awkward and amateurish, and then he jolted backwards and scared the shit out of me and I stumbled, and just as I was righting myself, my leg caught on the parapet and sent me flailing in the other direction.

Over the edge of the roof.

I remember screaming.

And I remember *not* falling.

I remember Arnaath's arms around me as he knelt on

the roof and cradled me to his chest. His body was warm and strong, his grip on me firm but gentle. And I remember wondering why he wasn't crouched on top of his perch as usual. He didn't speak. Didn't utter a single word. Just put me back on my feet, pressed a finger to his lips to shush me, then pointed to the ladder.

I was so stunned that I didn't even think to argue with him, just did as I was told—a rarity in and of itself —but when I snuck back up there after dinner, Arnaath was back in his usual spot. Crouched on top of the parapet, keeping a watchful eye on the graveyard and its inhabitants. And no matter what I did or said to him, he didn't budge, and when I'd tried telling my parents about it, they'd questioned my sanity and sold the house.

"Your skin is so soft," Arnaath whispers in my ear, his rich timbre drawing me back to the present. "Like the finest velvets, or a luxurious silk." His words hold a tone of wonderment. "I know you want me to fuck you, Chloe, but what I have in mind for you is so much more than mere fucking."

And now I'm staring up at him in wonderment. No one's ever promised me *that* before. "Arnaath, yes. Please." I tunnel my fingers through his hair, still amazed by how it moves, how real it feels. "I'm yours."

He shifts against me, settles his body more firmly between my thighs, and I gasp at the feel of his cock pressing against my belly. The heat of him is soothing, yet the weight of him excites. I'm not used to being outmatched in size. I'm used to being the aggressor, the assertive one, not too shy to tell a man what I want in or out of bed.

But Arnaath makes me feel special, small, almost delicate. I know he'll do what he promised. I know he'll take care of me.

He's always made me feel safe.

Now I know what it feels like to be wanted by him too.

His lips are hot as they travel down my throat in one open-mouthed kiss after another. I let my head fall back, granting him access to wherever he wants and moaning my appreciation of everywhere he's been. When he reaches my breasts, he sits back on his haunches and grins, licking his lips.

"So luscious," he murmurs, and in the blink of an eye, he has one nipple in his mouth, the other pinched between his fingers.

A sound escapes me that I barely recognise. Is it agony? Ecstasy? Pain or pleasure? I don't know. I don't care. I haven't had sex in over a year. Not since my mother told me I wasn't dreaming.

Not since she told me Arnaath was real.

All I've thought about since that day is getting back to him, and now I have. Now I'm here. And he's making my back arch in delight as he sucks one nipple, then the other, plucking with his lips, nibbling with his teeth. "Arn! Yes. More."

Lifting his head, he grins at me. "More?"

"Please," I moan and try to force his head back to my breasts. But he's far too strong for that.

He chuckles, low and predatory. "Greedy girl." He lowers his head again, and I feel him smile against my flesh as he grabs my tits in both hands and squishes them together. Why do guys always do that, try to make one giant boob? Considering Arnaath's age, I suppose it's nice to know it's nothing new.

When I feel his tongue snake around my nipples once

more, I let out a low moan and arch my back again. I don't know what he's doing to them, but I had no idea my breasts were so incredibly sensitive.

And all that sensitivity is spreading outwards, sliding through me, hunting for more. Building. Multiplying. Making me wet and needy.

Driving me crazy.

I want him inside me.

Chapter Five

A rnaath

Chloe writhes beneath me, her body undulating with unrestrained passion. "Arnaath, please."

I cup her cheek. "I've got you, love."

With one final kiss on each nipple, I continue downwards, between her breasts, over her stomach, then detour to her hip. Bite her soft flesh. Kiss her sweet skin. And all while gently stroking her everywhere.

I know it's making her crazy, but it's also making her wet. I can feel her arousal slick on her thighs, smell the musk of her as I draw closer to her quim.

She's more than ready for me.

Gazing into her pretty blue eyes, I draw back on my knees and take a moment to simply drink her in. Her hair is down and fanned out around her and just as sexy as I'd imagined, crowning her in a halo of burnished copper.

Her lips are plump and red from my kisses. Her skin is lightly tanned and freckled in some places, milky white in others, a testament to her life lived outdoors. Her long legs are strong and capable, her hands small and delicate.

Hands I wish to feel on my body again. Stroking my back as I fill her with my cock. Grabbing my arse and pulling me deeper as I fuck her hard and fast and make her scream my name.

Pulling my hair as I lick between her legs and take her to Heaven.

I smile wickedly, and she narrows her gaze. "What are you up to?"

"Something you'll enjoy," I tell her, then hook my hands behind her thighs and drag her into position, propping her arse up on an embroidered cushion worthy of a courtier's boudoir. Or a brothel. You'd be surprised how much overlap there is in that Venn diagram. "Are you ready, my lady?"

"Ready for what?"

I get in position and lick my lips. "This."

I revel in Chloe's squeal of delight as I go straight for her clit. That little bundle of nerves has been taunting me all evening, but I had left it untouched until now. I wanted to tease my lover instead, make her so crazy for my tongue, for my cock, that she'd explode the moment I entered her.

I wanted her so desirous for me that she'd never look at another man again.

Mine!

Chloe is mine at last, and I will give her the pleasure she craves.

Deserves.

I will devote my immortality to giving her orgasms beyond reckoning. To making her come and come and come.

She will know only happiness in my bed and in my arms.

"Arn," she moans. "Yes." She slides her fingers through my hair and digs her fingernails into my scalp.

That tiny bite of pain is all the encouragement I need, and I flick my tongue faster, suck her clit harder. Slip two fingers inside her. She's so wet, so hot and beautiful.

When Chloe cries out again, it's not the scream I'd anticipated but a husky moan of desire. Her back bows, lifting her arse off the cushion, forcing her body against my mouth.

I pump my fingers in and out of her, faster and faster, making her wetter and wetter. And I eat her perfect little cunt like the sweet treat it is until she's writhing like a wild thing, pulling my hair and coming all over my face.

So fucking sexy.

Her orgasm fades and she slumps back on the bed I made for her, scrunching the soft purple blanket in her hands even as her body still rides the aftershocks of her pleasure. Purple, the colour of royalty, of wealth and decadence. The colour suits her.

My lady, my princess.

My lover.

Her gaze catches mine, and I smile languidly, enjoying her expression of bliss and the gentle rise and fall of her chest as she sucks down air. "That was.... Wow. I don't even know how you're going to top that performance because that was.... *Fuck.* There are no words to describe how good that was."

I can't help the self-satisfied chuckle that escapes me or the purr of my voice as I assure her, "Believe me, princess, we're only just getting started." Then I crawl over the top of her, pin her down and take her mouth, let her taste herself on my lips and tongue.

She moans into my mouth, the sound one of surrender, and her hands slide down my body, exploring, searching.

Finding.

Her warm hand wraps around my cock, and I pump my hips forwards, fucking her palm. Then she guides me to her entrance, notches my dick against her slick heat and... waits.

She waits for me to take the lead, so I do.

With one slow thrust, I bury myself deep inside Chloe's body, enjoying the erotic glide of her quim against my cock. The heat that envelopes me makes the fire in the hearth seem a mere candle next to a furnace.

It cannot compare to the warmth that fills my body and soul as I make love to my woman.

And I thought I felt powerful before.

What I feel now is ten times more potent. A hundred times more. And as I gaze down on Chloe's face, as I watch her eyelids shutter and listen to her whimper and moan as I fill her over and over again, I know I will never feel this way with anyone else.

I was created over seven hundred years ago, carved from marble and imbued with magic I do not understand, and all for the pleasure of others. I was their plaything, their toy, and yes, I took my pleasure in them too. But nothing like this.

Nothing so rapturous.

Nothing and no one as euphoric as the feel of Chloe under me, surrounding me.

Loving me.

My sweet, sexy, weird Chloe.

A woman worthy of praise, deserving of my worship. But I can't worship her from above.

In a move that has us both gasping and groaning, I flip us over so I'm on my back and she's straddling me, riding me.

Enjoying the fuck out of me, as is her due.

Leaning forwards, she places her palms flat against my chest and stares down at me. One corner of her mouth lifts in a small smile, secretive and yet not. But that was always her way, showing the world just enough of herself, keeping the rest private. Letting in only those she deemed worthy. Weirdos like her.

Weirdos like me.

The way I look doesn't bother her. Not my wings or my broken pieces or my mismatched eyes. Perhaps because that's how she has always seen me, but knowing she accepts me as I am, as I do her, is almost as mind-blowing as the orgasm I feel building in the base of my spine.

"Chloe, love." My voice is harsh, and I tighten my grip on her hips as she moves her pelvis in one continuous, tortuous rolling motion. "*Fuck.*"

I dare not break eye contact with her. I don't want to miss a single thing, not one single emotion as they flit and dance through her gaze. So I watch her, enraptured by her movements, enthralled by her expressions, and enchanted by her smile. That sweet, serene smile that spreads to fill her whole face as her head tips back and her breathing quickens.

Her fingernails dig into my abs. "Arnaath," she moans. "I want to— I'm going to— Ah, *fuck,* Arnaath! I'm going to come!"

"Yes, love. Come for me. Show me your passion."

But there's no screaming for my Chloe.

Just as before, her orgasm makes itself known in a

gentler fashion. There's no yelling, no thrashing, no exclamations to the heavens above. No, when my lover comes, she does so quietly, reverently, and with her teeth sunk so far into her bottom lip I'm afraid she'll bite right through it.

When her body shakes with her climax, when she clamps down on my own flesh and squeezes with superhuman force, a riot of sensation explodes through my body too. Spears outwards from the base of my spine until it infuses every inch of me with feeling, with heat and lust and an unending sense of awe.

And a strong desire to do it all over again.

Chloe relaxes and I know she is spent—I fucking am—but even so, when she collapses on top of me, she peppers my body and face with quick little kisses. Until I catch her chin in my hand and bring her mouth to mine, slip my tongue between her teeth and taste her once more.

Revel in her.

Worship her.

"Thank you," she murmurs.

"It was my pleasure," I assure her.

She pokes her finger into my side, making me smile. "Not that. I meant thank you for saving me. I never said it to you, and I should have."

I pull her closer and kiss the top of her head. "That was my pleasure too."

I was built to pleasure women, to fawn over them and pamper them and treat them with care and respect.

Never did I think I'd fall in love with one.

Not until Chloe came into my life, then almost fell out of it.

I know I should end this, should push her away. I know the day will come when she will die and I will slowly fade back into the stone from whence I came, but until that day comes to pass, I have a rock-hard cock, a libido that will not be ignored, and a willing woman in my arms.

My woman.

Mine.

BATTERY

OPERATED

BOYFRIEND

For my readers, you gorgeous, kinky people.

Chapter One

R *emus*

"Turn right in three, two, one, now."

Moving as quickly as I dare, I follow the instructions being fed through my earpiece, trusting my IT and comms specialist, Tech, to direct me to the target safely and without incident.

Our orders came down a few days ago.

We're to audit one of our government contractors, which is just a fancy way of saying we need to sneak in, check they're doing everything by the book and not creating unsanctioned weapons of mass destruction, and report back to HQ with our findings.

Man, I hope we find something.

Our preliminary search turned up nothing but redacted files. Not completely unheard of but not exactly above board either. But when Tech dug a little deeper, he found references to a Dr J. Johnson, and something called Project Pork Sword.

For fuck's sake. My eyes rolled so hard when I read that I think I saw the back of my brain. But that's what happens when you let virgins name things.

Christ only knows what Project—

Nope. I'm not calling it that.

Christ only knows what the project is. The fact some idiot named it after his dick tells me everything I need to know about the idiot and absolutely nothing about the project.

We need to know what these arseholes are up to. We need to know if those redacted files are something to worry about or just the work of an overzealous intern.

We need to get this shit done so I can go home and feed my cat.

"Follow this hallway to the end, then turn left. Follow that hallway to the end and you should see your target. Bio Lab Three."

"The dead zone," I murmur, tugging my cap lower to avoid eye contact with a woman coming towards me, pushing a cleaning cart.

"Exactly. Once you enter the dead zone, you'll be on your own. It's completely shielded from all surveillance, so no comms in or out. No cameras either. You'll be going in completely blind."

The hallways are virtually empty now, but they won't be for long. Shift change is about to happen, and if our intel is correct, I should be able to slip inside the dead zone with little to no interference during the changeover. Blend into the crowd.

That's the main reason I'm in here instead of one of my men. I'm exceedingly average. Not at my job—I'm a decorated soldier, for fuck's sake. But to look at, certainly.

Average height, average build, a little grey sneaking into my otherwise brown hair, and a borderline ugly face, but not so much as to make me stand out.

My only identifying mark is one barbed-wire tattoo wrapped around my bicep, the remnant of a night out when I was young and stupid and too drunk to realise my mates had poured me into the tattooist's chair until the pain started, and that's hidden—along with a small arsenal—under my stolen guard's uniform.

Anyone watching me wouldn't know anything was amiss. Except for my boots. Because the only thing about me that isn't average is my shoe size, and the guard I rendered unconscious so I could steal his clothes had dainty feet. Not that I'm overly worried about anyone seeing my combat boots. People rarely think to look at other people's feet.

Waiting until the woman has passed me by before whispering, "Acknowledged," I turn down the hallway that leads to my target. A brief siren sounds overhead, signalling the shift change, and the hallway quickly fills with people spilling out of one lab and heading to wherever the fuck they need to go, their heads down and their steps hurried. As long as they don't prevent me from doing my job, I don't give a fuck where they go.

Keeping my gaze fixed ahead of me, I paste on my best resting dick face and move through the crowded hallway. People quickly move out of my way, their gazes averted as if scared of what will happen should they look directly at me. Handy, since I don't want to be identified, but I also find it worrisome they fear the people who are supposed to be protecting them. That's not normal.

Gritting my teeth against a spike of sudden anger, I remind myself it's also not my problem. Not right now. I make a mental note to add it to my report.

Stay on mission.

Nearing my destination, I check my surroundings again. No one is paying me any attention, so I tap my comms twice to give the signal.

Tech's quiet murmur fills my earpiece. "When the cameras go offline, you'll have ten seconds to get through the door before they re-engage. Good luck, Colonel." He counts me down, then says, "Go. Now."

The access keypad in front of me uses bio-identification. Luckily, my team is skilled in acquiring such identification and manufacturing exactly what I need to complete my mission, like a fake handprint. Ten seconds isn't much time, just enough to key in the security code and press my palm to the scanner. In a few seconds, I'll either be on the other side of this door or in a fuckload of trouble.

A soft beep followed by a quiet *snick* as the door unlocks causes me to send up a silent prayer of thanks to the powers that be. And Tech. Mostly Tech. "Going dark."

I slip inside the room.

Enter the unknown.

A quiet crackle of static sounds through my earpiece, and then all is silence. I'm on my own from here on out.

Now the real work begins.

Gather intelligence. Collect samples. And, if the opportunity presents itself, pump Dr Johnson for as much information as possible.

Turning to face the room, I'm surprised to find it empty. Where are the scientists? Where are the lab techs? This is supposed to be a hub of activity, the heart of BioAID's secret weapons division. So where did everybody go?

My eyes narrow. There's something wrong with this situation.

Reaching into the back of my uniform, I palm my service pistol and begin my sweep of the room.

This place is a ghost town.

Maybe our intelligence is incorrect, or incomplete?

Maybe I'm in the wrong lab?

Shit.

Where is everyone?

The lab has all the usual hallmarks found in places like this: bright white walls, harsh fluorescent lighting and stainless-steel benches everywhere I look. But the machines are eerily quiet, some covered in plastic sheeting.

Many of the work areas are empty, but some are filled with tools and what looks like electrical diagnostic equipment. One bench is lined with prosthetic arms, another with hands and feet. And on one bench, under a thin sheet of plastic, there appears to be what looks like... I wanna say sex toys...?

Edging closer, I see that, yep, it's a table full of cocks. And I'm not talking about your standard, everyday, run-of-the-mill dildos here either.

I mean *cocks.*

Long, thick, porno-sized dicks.

And unlike the arms, hands, and feet—I swallow hard to choke down the bile rising in my throat—the dicks look real.

What in the ever-loving fuck is going on here?

I'd be lying if I say my balls haven't shrunk to the size of raisins at the grizzly sight, but as much as I don't really want to look at a bunch of dismembered members, it's my job to investigate everything, to look at things from every angle.

Take samples as evidence.

Though I have to admit, what a table covered in dicks might be evidence of eludes me.

A shudder runs up my spine as I gingerly lift the thin sheet of plastic and try not to recoil at the sight of several severed cocks. After slipping my pistol back in its holster, I reach into one of my pockets to retrieve and pull on a pair of latex gloves, then pick up the dick most likely to fit in my pocket. One small enough that I can smuggle it out of here. I can't help the way my lips pull back in disgust—it's a severed penis, for fuck's sake—but then I notice something curious.

It's heavy.

Much heavier than I thought a human cock would be. Especially for its size.

Turning it over in my hand, I take a closer look and realise the flesh, as real as it looks and feels, isn't. This isn't a real dick. My relief is palpable and escapes me on a shuddering breath.

To test my theory, I tap it against the edge of the metal table. Laugh at the thudding sound it makes. "Prosthetic dicks? How would they even work?"

Okay. Consider my curiosity piqued. But prosthetic body parts weren't exactly what I thought I'd find in here. And they're certainly not worth all that redacted paper.

Slipping the misappropriated appendage in my pocket, I palm my weapon again and move towards the door set in the far wall.

A sudden noise comes from beyond the door. A loud *thud* followed by a woman cursing, like she'd been hurt.

My guardian instincts go on high alert. No one hurts a woman on my watch.

Testing the door handle, I find it's unlocked and slip through to the other room as quickly and quietly as possible.

What I find on the other side is even more bizarre than the lab I just left.

And infinitely more fuckable.

Fuck me. I think I'm in love.

Chapter Two

J*enna*

"ARGH! YOU PIECE-OF-SHIT ARSEHOLE! WHY?"

As the couplers on the latest prototype fail to engage —*again*—and B.O.B.'s shiny new enhancement falls limply to the floor with a dull *thud*—*again*—I restrain the urge to kick him.

Firstly, violence never solved anything.

And secondly, the last time I kicked him, I broke my toe.

But that's what happens when you build state-of-the-art robotics that could pass for a human being in a pinch. Occasionally you forget they're not real and kick them in the shins.

Maybe if I wasn't so good at my job I wouldn't have. Of course, if I wasn't so damn good at my job, BioAID wouldn't have recruited me. And by "recruited", I mean kidnapped at gunpoint and forced to sign over my life's work.

B.O.B.

My Bio-Organic Body.

Creating affordable prosthetic body parts for the world's most vulnerable citizens—people like my little sister —that's where my heart lies. And not just limbs either, legs, arms, hands, feet. I wanted to make artificial organs too. Hearts, lungs, kidneys. And yes, even cocks.

B.O.B. is the culmination of my life's work. Countless hours of research and development, endless cups of coffee, and sleepless nights. Dinners missed, dates broken. And on the rare occasions I did make it home from the lab, a cold, empty bed waiting for me in my apartment.

Sad to think not much has changed really.

Except I didn't get into this gig to build sex-bots.

I wasn't able to help my little sister beat lung disease, and I saw what her death did to my parents, how it ripped them apart. But imagine the lives that could be saved if people didn't have to wait on transplant lists. Imagine if hospitals everywhere had a steady supply of whatever they needed to help their patients.

No more waiting to find someone with a perfect blood match. No more waiting for someone else to die and hoping they were a donor.

More people living their lives the way they want to.

At least, that was the dream.

Until BioAID's CEO, a nasty little pervert named Rowly Thorne, decided that instead of helping heal humanity, my robotics would be much better off making him bank. As sex-bots. A basic B.O.B. sells for thirty-five grand. A customised model sells for upwards of seventy.

Why? Because my robots are the only kind in existence that function much like a human being does, and they can be programmed to do pretty much anything. Even kiss. With tongue.

B.O.B. 2.0

The Battery-Operated Boyfriend.

Picking the bot's new cock up off the floor, I let loose another growl of frustration. "Why aren't you working?"

I have to give the board a demonstration in fifteen minutes, and if I can't fix the problem, I'll have nothing to show them, which is not a situation I want to find myself in again.

The last time I failed, they took away my outdoor recreation time for two months. Figured I needed to focus more on my work than my tan. In retaliation, I tried escaping again. As retribution they added an extra month to my punishment.

I should have known I wouldn't get far. I might be able to hack my way through most security systems, but I suck at being sneaky. They caught me before I'd even hit the call button for the elevators.

And then they changed my security, adding bio-identification to the main entry so I couldn't hack my way out again.

That was over a year ago.

Even if I could hack the bio-identity bullshit, why bother?

It's not like there's anyone left to miss me. My family are all gone, and as for friends, well, I never really had any of those to begin with. No girl gang. Certainly not a boyfriend.

Work always came first.

I'm forty-two years old and completely alone. But I don't have time to wallow in my doldrums. I have work to do.

Always fucking work.

Sighing, I turn the attachment over in my hands. I can find no good reason for it not to work. My top lab techs have been working on these damn things for months, perfecting them, I thought.

Crouching down, I inspect the connection site instead. Poke around in his groin. To anyone watching, it would look like I'm giving him a blow job. The observation has been made before. Usually right before I fire someone.

"Maybe you have a loose wire," I muse. "Or maybe the connector is faulty." I scratch my head, thinking through the problem. "It could be a software issue, I suppose. There has to be a reason the—"

The door to my personal quarters opens and closes. It's quiet, barely discernible over the hum of the air filtration system and soft lounge music playing on my stereo, but it's there.

Someone is there. Behind me.

Someone who shouldn't be there, because I gave everyone the day off today. Like I always do on demonstration days.

Slowly, I push up off the floor and try to remain cool and casual as I look around for a weapon, but there's nothing. Even if I was strong enough to remove one of B.O.B.'s arms on my own, it would take too long. The intruder would be on me before I even opened the access port.

As I turn around, I try not to think about the fact I'm wearing nothing but my underwear and a tank top. And not even my cute underwear but my dodgy-as-fuck, stretched-out cotton underwear I keep around in case of an emergency. Like this morning when I realised I hadn't done my laundry for two weeks and this was the last pair of clean undies I owned.

Frankly, the tank top has seen better days too. I swear, last week the hole sitting just above my right breast was the size of a pinhead. Now it's more like a gaping tear and threatening to flash my nipple to the world.

I didn't think much of it when I got dressed this morning. Probably because I knew it was coming off again before lunch.

Honestly, I look more like I just crawled off a deserted island than the award-winning biomechanical engineer I actually am.

"Who are you? What is this place?" he says, then nods at B.O.B. "And what the fuck is that thing?" Deep and commanding, the intruder's voice sounds like he routinely gargles gravel. It's hot as fuck and—

Daaamn. He is hot as fuck.

When I face him fully, I can't help the breath I suck back as my gaze catches his, the one that sticks in my lungs before shuddering out of me again. Velvety and rich, his dark eyes roam around my room, taking everything in—my dresser, the open door to my bathroom, the pile of dirty clothes in the corner, the bed. Then he settles his gaze on me. His expression is curious. Cautious... yet interested.

Aroused.

I'm confident I know what he's feeling, because I've been studying micro-expressions for years, programming them into my bots to make them more realistic, and I'm very good at what I do. I've studied that look down to the minutest detail. I'm intimate with it. I'm turned on by it. I feel my cheeks heat.

"Well?" he demands, snapping his arms out in front of him like he's just remembered he's supposed to be doing something other than staring at my tits. And that's when I notice the gun he has trained on me.

I haven't had a gun pointed at me in a long time. Not since I was brought to this hellhole.

What do I do?

I can't remember.

What do I say?

My mouth feels dry. My feet have frozen to the floor, and no sound is coming out of my gaping maw.

"Look at me," he says, his tone softer than before but by no means less commanding.

I am totally freaking out, but I can't not look at the gun in his big hands. And my brain is going crazy imagining that soft voice whispering filthy things in my ear, and those big hands all over my body as he fucks me hard and—

Oh my God, I am losing my mind.

But this is what happens when you're not allowed to leave the building for months at a time, and even then, only under guard. Not to mention the fact I've not had sex with another human being in... I don't even remember how long.

Years. It's been years.

Shit like that makes a girl *slightly* insane.

Shit. For all I know, this guy is here to kill me, and what am I doing? I'm desperately trying not to squeeze my thighs together and give away the fact he's making me horny as hell.

Oh, what I wouldn't give to feel his tongue in my pussy right now.

Sweet Jesus, Jenna. Get a grip.

Swallowing hard against the crazy fear/lust combo clogging my throat, I'm almost positive that's the only thing stopping me from screaming right now. And what did he ask me? My poor brain is overwhelmed, confused. Irritated.

I'm supposed to demonstrate B.O.B.'s latest upgrades in less than fifteen minutes' time. Or else. Except none of them work, I'm completely stressing out, I'm tired, and now I'm being held at gunpoint by some random guy I can't stop undressing in my mind. I'm so close to tears it's embarrassing.

And I'm not a crier.

I'm just so *exhausted*.

"Miss? I'm going to put the gun away, okay?"

I didn't realise I'd stopped looking at the hot killer guy until his voice drew my attention again. And... *wow*. He really is sexy.

There really is something wrong with me.

My mystery man is of average height and a stockier build than most of the men around here, scientists and security guards alike. I tilt my head slightly, narrow my gaze on his clothes. It's definitely one of BioAID's uniforms, but it's a little tight across his chest, shoulders, and thighs, almost as though it belongs to someone else. His black combat boots aren't regulation either, not that many would notice.

Fascinating.

His ill-fitting uniform has the advantage of showing off his physique. His musculature is impressive, as is the bulge in his trousers.

But... that can't be right.

Not unless he has two—

Leaning forwards, I narrow my gaze on his crotch as realisation dawns, and my shoulders tighten in anger. Cocking one brow, I snarl, "Is that a bionic penis in your pocket, or are you just happy to see me?"

Sexy killer man is a thief.

Chapter Three

R *emus*

I CAN'T HELP the burst of laughter that explodes out of me as my sexy little companion bends over to stare at my dick, and the way she snarls at me is so fucking cute. She's like a curvy little wildcat, all spit and fire, and suddenly an image of her scratching up my back as I fuck her senseless fills my mind and hardens my cock.

This mission is turning out to be a weird one, but I am not complaining.

Not if it means getting to know this fascinating woman better.

Tucking my weapon back in its holster, I raise my hands in a placating gesture, but instead of diffusing the situation, she continues glaring at me.

"What's your name?" she demands, straightening, her

hands anchoring to her soft, wide hips. "How did you get in here?"

I'm the one who's supposed to be asking the questions, but that tear in her shirt, the one begging me to hook my fingers through it and rip it wider, exposing her soft breasts to my eager mouth and wet tongue, is so damn distracting that I answer her without thinking.

"You can call me Remus," I say, removing my cap and shoving it in my back pocket.

"*Call* you Remus?" The wildcat raises one brow at me and folds her arms over her ample chest. "Is that your real name?"

I'm trained to withstand interrogation, to keep intel to myself until death if need be, but this woman is so damn intriguing, and the situation so fucking weird, that I can't stop having a little fun with her. "It's the only one you're getting, sweetheart, so I suggest we move on to who *you* are, what that is, and what the hell you're doing here dressed like... *that*."

A sudden flicker of shame crosses her pretty face, and she drops her arms, tugs at the hem of her shirt, and pulls it lower. Then in an instant she's spitting fire at me again, glaring at me. "You shouldn't be here. No one is allowed to be here. Not today. And especially not you."

I cock one brow. "Why not me?" I ask, inching ever closer to where she stands. I need to go slow, make my movements as small as possible so I don't spook her any further. Keep her calm. Stop her from escaping. Not that it looks like she has anywhere to go, and certainly not dressed like that. "Why not today?"

"You're a thief." She spits the accusation at me.

"I'm not a th—"

"Your uniform doesn't fit you, you're wearing the wrong

type of boots, and unless you've been blessed with *two* enormous dicks, that's one of my prototypes in your pocket," she snaps at me, then huffs and folds her arms again. "And anyone who actually works here knows the last Friday of every quarter is my demonstration day with the board and has the good sense to stay the fuck out of my lab, else they get fired. Now," she says, lifting her chin and flicking her gaze to the clock on the wall, "would you kindly take my dick out of your pants and leave?" Her eyes, clear and sharp, come back to mine. "I have work to do."

What work could she possibly have to do in her underwear?

My gaze snags on the thing standing behind her. It looks like a man, but not exactly like a man. It's too... perfect. Real men are anything but perfect.

Reaching into my pocket, I grab the mechanical cock and pull it free, look at it, look at the man, take in the glassy eyes and not quite natural facial expression.

"Is this his?" I ask, holding up the dick.

Her lips purse. She's irritated. "One of them."

She lunges forwards and tries to take the appendage from my hand, but I hold it over our heads. She's quick, I'll give her that. But not quick enough. She makes a growly sound at the back of her throat and I grin at her. Fuck, she's sexy. Small and curvy with sweetly bowed lips and intelligent eyes framed by impossibly long lashes.

My cock keeps twitching, distracting me, urging me to yank this woman into my arms, fist my hands in the mess of her blonde wavy hair and kiss her until her toes curl and we make use of the bed behind her. But business first. There is something very strange going on here, and I need to know what it is.

I have work to do too.

When her gaze darts to the clock again, my grin fades. "What's your name?"

Turning back to her overgrown toy, she says, "I don't have time for this."

Shoving the cock back in my pocket, I grab her shoulders and turn her around, force her to face me. "Make time."

Teeth gritted together, she hisses out a breath. "Jenna. I'm Dr Jenna Johnson. I run this lab."

I narrow my gaze as I take another, slower look at her. There was nothing in the files describing Dr Johnson, not even their sex, so it's completely possible I'm looking for a woman. "Jenna spelled with a J?"

She snorts. "Obviously."

Great. Dr J. Johnson. Jenna. The wildcat dressed in her underwear and spitting fire at me is the lead scientist on the bioweapons project.

Because of course she is.

I finally find a woman who's cute, fiery, and sexy as fuck, and she's in charge of the project I'm here to audit.

Fuck my life.

"Why do you keep looking at the clock?" I want her focus on me. "What are you waiting for?"

That shadow of shame flickers over her sweet face again before she lifts her chin and glares at me. "First tell me who you are and what you're really doing here. Are you a competitor? A saboteur? What? And be quick, please. I'm on a schedule."

Jenna's urgent tone and nervous gaze wouldn't usually be enough to convince me to tell her who I really am, but the way she keeps looking at that damn clock is strange, and one of my objectives is to turn key staff members into informants if possible. And it doesn't get more key than the scientist in charge of the whole fucking project.

"All right. I'm a colonel in charge of a special division of the Department of Defence. My team periodically investigates the defence contractors we work with and makes sure they're following the letter of the law. BioAID was red-flagged for suspicious activity in regard to a Project Pork Sword," I tell her, barely refraining from rolling my eyes, "and your lab was at the centre of that activity."

"What suspicious activity?"

"Illegal weapons. Specifically bioweapons."

Jenna stares at me, her eyes wide and her mouth slack, then bursts out laughing. "Bioweapons," she repeats, doubled over, wrapping her arms around her middle. "The only bioweapon around here is the one you shoved in your pocket."

"What?"

"We don't make weapons, Colonel," she says, wiping tears of laughter from her cheeks. "We make sex-bots. High-end, luxury sex-bots. Or, as I call him," she says, indicating the thing behind her, "B.O.B."

The irony lifts one corner of my mouth in a sardonic grin. "Bob?"

Her laughter fades. "You know." She groans, her cheeks pinkening with embarrassment. "Battery-Operated—"

"Yeah," I say, holding my hand up to stop her explanation. "I know what it stands for."

Jesus. I need to sit down. I have so many questions. But before I can ask any of them, Jenna's mouth falls open and she stares at me intently, running her intelligent gaze over me from head to toe and back again.

"You're with defence," she says quietly, almost as if she's

talking to herself. Then she steps closer and fists her hands in my shirtfront, staring up at me, desperation written all over her face. "You can get me out of here. You can help me escape."

Escape? Frowning, I settle my hands on her shoulders and push her back slightly so I can see her face, read her expression. "What do you mean? You're being held against your will?"

"Yes!" She presses her body closer, and I smell the floral scent of her shampoo. The proximity of her soft body and the feminine scent in her hair make my dick twitch. *Focus, arsehole. She needs your help.* "The people running this place are insane," she says. "Perverted and insane." She looks at the clock again, then back at me and chews on her bottom lip.

Dr Johnson is either a very good liar or she's telling the truth. I don't detect any deceit in her tone or body language. "Tell me what happened. How did you come to be here?"

Jenna nods, takes a breath, then talks fast. "Three years ago, my research into prosthetics was making waves in all the right ways, but I needed funding. BioAID stepped up. They said they would fund my research if I came to work for them, but their contracts were terrible. They wanted full ownership of all my patents, past, present, and future, so I turned them down. No way was I letting them take full control of my intellectual property. Next thing I know, there are masked men with guns in my house, telling me to pack a bag and come with them. What was I supposed to do?"

Her earlier nervousness and shame make sense to me now, and I want to wrap my arms around her and pull her body flush against mine, comfort her. It would be so easy to get lost in her soft curves and warm skin, but I don't. I can't. Instead, I tighten my hands on her shoulders and squeeze.

I reassure her. Like a good soldier. "You did the right thing, Jenna. You survived."

"When I got here, the CEO, Mr Thorne, he told me he was going to use my inventions to change the world. He said he would fund my research into prosthetics as long as I allowed BioAID to use B.O.B. to dominate the sex-bot market. And at first he did, but the more money B.O.B. made, the more he restricted my research. Now the bots are the *only* thing I'm allowed to work on." She scoffs and shakes her head. "I used to be proud of what I did for a living. I made life-saving devices and gave people hope. Now I make walking vibrators and give bored, rich house-wives orgasms."

It doesn't happen often, but I am at a loss for words. When I find my voice again, I say, "So, if I understand you correctly, Thorne had you kidnapped and held here at BioAID so he could use your invention to make high-end sex-bots, not bioweapons?"

Jenna scowls at my obvious bewilderment but nods. "It's a very lucrative market."

"And you've been here for three years?"

"Yes! And I want out of here." She tightens her grip on my shirt before shooting another furtive glance at the clock. "Please. I just wanna go home."

I shove my fingers through my hair, still unsure what to think about any of this. "First tell me about this demonstra-tion you have to give. And what's with the ticking clock?"

Brow furrowed in a look of concentration, Jenna lets go of my shirt and starts pressing her fingertips against my chest, feeling my abs, then pastes on an unnaturally broad smile. "Funny you should ask."

Uh-oh.

Chapter Four

J *enna*

"Do you have a hairy chest?"

"What?"

"Hairy. Chest," I repeat slowly, deliberately. I don't have time for him to question my every move, even the absolutely, 100 percent batshit insane ones. "Yes or no?"

Remus frowns and slowly shakes his head. "Ah, no."

"Abs?"

His eyes shoot wide. "Excuse me?"

"I mean, you feel pretty solid under here. It's quite impressive," I say, ignoring his reaction and the way he subtly thrusts his hips towards me as I continue blindly exploring his powerful chest, "but would you say you're cut, jacked, or ripped?"

Now he just looks confused. Grabbing my wrists, he removes my hands from his body, but he doesn't push me away. That's encouraging at least, especially considering what I'm about to suggest to the good colonel. The incredibly sexy, hot, manly colonel.

The quickly getting annoyed colonel. "What is happening right now? Why are you so interested in my chest?"

"Not just your chest." I step back from his warm presence and force a laugh to lighten the mood. It doesn't work. "I had an idea. It's completely insane and probably won't work, but here goes."

Before I can chicken out, I yank my tank top over my head and toss it on the floor, then take advantage of Remus's confusion and throw myself at him, hoping he's just like every other man out there: horny and opportunistic.

Just my luck, I get the one and only gentleman. Or maybe I misread him earlier and he wasn't staring at my tits? Either way, before my lips get anywhere near his, he gently sets me away from him.

"Oh, sweetheart, you don't have to do that," he says, his gravelly voice softening as he takes off his shirt and drapes it around me. As tight as the garment was on him, it dwarfs me. Remus pulls the edges together, hiding my body completely. "I'll help you. You have my word."

His compassion makes my knees weak and tears threaten to spill down my cheeks, but I don't have time to feel this way.

That damn clock is ticking away, and time is running out.

"You don't understand," I tell him, trying very hard not to snap at this man who has shown me my first drop of kindness in over three years. "The demonstration—" This is so humiliating. "I don't just have to show the board members my new designs," I say, feeling my whole body flush with embarrassment. "I have to... prove viability of concept."

Remus's gaze darts to B.O.B., then back to me, his dark eyes wide and his lips parting in shock. "I'm pretty sure I know what that means, but put it in plain English for me anyway, just to make sure I understand you completely."

I moisten my lips and stare up at him, swallow hard. "I have to have sex with B.O.B."

His nostrils flare. "And they *watch* while you do this?" he growls, his eyes narrowing to slits, disgust written clearly across his face.

I hang my head in shame. "Yes."

"Jesus Christ," he mutters, and even while looking down, I can see him anchor his hands on his hips, his thick fingers flexing. "Well I guess that explains all the redacted files we found. Kidnapping, unlawful imprisonment, and... I'm not even sure what to call this," he says, waving a hand at B.O.B. "If this ever got out, it would bankrupt them." Warm fingers cup my cheek and lift my face until I'm staring up at him again. "So let's make that happen," he says, his smile reassuring. "Let's get out of here."

For a moment, I'm so caught up in Remus's sexy grin and bright eyes that I almost forget what's about to happen, forget my idea, but then my survival instincts kick back in and I shake my head. "We can't go. Not yet."

Remus folds his arms over his expansive chest. His biceps threaten to rip through the sleeves of his undershirt. "Why?"

"The demonstration. If I'm not here for it, they'll lock down the entire facility until I'm found. Only, I can't give the demonstration because I couldn't attach B.O.B.'s new... ah, equipment."

He scratches his head. "Sweetheart, I can't help you with that."

"Actually, you can. That's why I was so interested in your chest. And the rest of you," I say, my cheeks near bursting into flame they're so damn hot. "Listen, I know what I'm about to propose is crazy and completely inappropriate, but it'll buy us time."

"Oh?" One dark brown brow wings up over those mesmerising eyes.

"You can be B.O.B."

A burst of laughter escapes him, but then he frowns. "You're serious?"

"Do you have a better idea?"

"Yeah. Tell them you need more time. Tell them there's an issue with the new equipment."

I shake my head. "I can't. Any failures on my part are dealt with swiftly."

"Meaning?"

"Meaning Thorne will send security to ransack my room and remove anything deemed a luxury or a distraction, anything that could possibly pull my focus away from my primary concern. Making him money," I add before he can ask, then look at the clock for what feels like the millionth time in the last ten minutes. *Shit*. Has it really been ten minutes since Remus snuck in here? Shaking my head, I back away. "I don't have time to argue this. The show starts in less than five minutes." Then I whisper, "Please help me get out of here."

Remus closes his eyes and shakes his head, sinks his teeth into his bottom lip, then slowly lets it slip free. It's sexy as fuck and makes me wish I'd met him under better circumstances. Maybe in a pub on a Saturday night, or at a barbeque with mutual friends. You know, if I ever went out, or had friends.

Then he laughs again, only it's more of a chuckle this time, and the next thing I know his arms are around me and he's hugging me tight and nuzzling my cheek, teasing my skin with his feather-light touch. "Okay, sweetheart. I promise I'll get you out," he purrs. "Right after I get you off."

My breath leaves me on a massive sigh of relief. "Thank you."

Immediately, he steps back again and reverts to soldier mode. "Tell me what you need."

"Hide him, his cock, and your weapons in the bathroom," I say, thumbing over my shoulder at B.O.B. "And be careful!" I add as Remus picks the bot up like it weighs nothing at all and dumps him in my tiny bathroom. "That's my life's work you're manhandling."

He shuts the bathroom door and stares at me for a moment, then says, "You know we can't take him with us, right?"

"Yeah, I figured as much," I say, sighing, then shrug. "Good thing I have everything stored on a backup drive."

Remus smirks. "Okay. What now?"

Slipping my arms through the sleeves of the shirt Remus draped around me, I don't bother to button it up—it's all coming off in a couple minutes anyway—but it makes it easier to talk to him like this.

"Well, obviously you look very different from the bots they're used to seeing, so I'm going to have to sell them on my new design, as it were. Which means I need to know what you look like. Under your clothes." When his eyebrows slide up again and those distracting lips form an even more distracting grin, I grit my teeth and straighten my spine. Now is not the time to be caught off guard. "Look, I need to know what you look like under your clothes, because if I describe you wrong, they're either going to think I'm an idiot or they'll realise something's up. And I can tell you now, they know I'm not an idiot. So, what am I working with here?"

Remus's grin widens, like he finds the entire situation ridiculously amusing—it's spectacularly sexy, if I'm being honest, that he can take all this in his stride and not freak out—then quickly and efficiently unfastens his trousers and pulls up his undershirt.

Saliva pools in my mouth as he reveals a hairless stomach packed with solid-looking muscle. Jacked. He's definitely jacked. His upper chest is also hair-free and taut. His skin is tanned, his nipples small and brown and flat. I want to lick them. Bite them.

As if they have a mind of their own, my thighs press together and my clit throbs. I know it's too much to hope he didn't notice my movements when his gaze flicks down my body and his grin slowly morphs into a sensual smile.

Fuck. Me.

The urge to throw myself at this man again is getting stronger by the second.

I mentally slap myself. *Down, girl. Now's not the time.*

Next he opens the flaps of his trousers and shoves down the front of his briefs. The sight that greets me has my jaw on the floor and my pulse racing like its training for the Olympics.

Ho. Ly. Shit.

His cock. Oh my fucking Lord, his cock.

As Remus wraps his meaty fist around the hard, thick length jutting out from between his thighs, my mouth runs dry, and I have to swallow hard against the emotion stuck in my throat. What is wrong with me? I work with dicks every other day of the week. Bigger dicks even than the one I'm currently staring at like a condemned man stares at his last meal.

But all I can think about is reaching out and touching him, stroking my fingers along his steely length of perfection and gripping him tight. Pulling him towards me, towards the bed. Lying back and letting him have his way with me.

Geez, I need to get laid.

By a man, not a machine.

Because it really doesn't matter how damn good I am at my job. There is no substitute for the feel of real flesh, heated by real blood and powered by a real heart. My fingers rub at the base of my throat as if of their own accord, a sexual response I can't seem to control.

I want him.

I want Remus.

"Seen enough?" he asks in that deliciously growly voice that does nothing to hide his humour. "Because if you keep staring at me like that, we're gunna start this show early."

I swallow thickly and turn away to hide my growing desire—and the growing wet patch in my panties—then take a desperately needed breath. "Yes. Thank you. You can get dressed."

I am in so much trouble.

Chapter Five

R *emus*

JENNA FINISHES EXPLAINING what will be expected during the demonstration, and the more she tells me, the more my blood boils. She's not even a person to these arse-holes, just a thing, a tool to be used to make money.

I can't wait to crush these bastards.

With only seconds to go before the show starts, she leans towards me and whispers, "I hope to hell you're not a selfish lover, or you'll blow your cover well before you blow your load."

"Is that a challenge?" I murmur softly, fighting to keep my expression neutral.

Goddamn but I want to put this woman on her hands and knees and fuck the sass right out of her. And then I want to flip her on her back and do it all over again. And in another minute or two, I just might get that chance.

At the stroke of 11:00 a.m. precisely, a large panel on one wall of her room slides up to reveal an equally large window and the room behind it, slightly elevated so they're looking down on us. A viewing platform.

Seven men and five women fill the room, all either wearing an expensive suit or a lab coat over their clothes. The people in lab coats carry digital tablets with them. The people in suits are drinking coffee and eating sandwiches like they're at a goddamn company picnic.

Their indifferent attitudes make me want to take Jenna's prosthetic cocks and shove them up their collective arses. Then I feel her fingertips brush against mine, and I want to grab her hand and run. But she's right. The only way out of here is to buy ourselves more time. And the only way to do that is to have sex in front of a roomful of perverts.

For science!

Yeah, right.

I want to look at Jenna. I want to make sure she's okay, tell her something reassuring, hold her. But I can't. I have to stand perfectly still and pretend to be a fucking sex-bot. Thank God for basic training, and for standing on parade for hours on end, and for a lifetime of not squirming while being scrutinised by my superior officers.

If anyone can pull this off, it's a soldier.

Jenna clears her throat to get everyone's attention. "Good morning, everyone, and welcome to today's demonstration."

Everyone moves closer to the window. Three of the men and one of the women leer at her. I can't say I blame them, but it still pisses me off. She'd ditched the shirt and underwear and stood beside me now in a pristine white lab coat and not a stitch of anything underneath. It's hot as fuck, and when I get her out of here, it's definitely something we'll be revisiting in the privacy of my own home.

Right now though, I just want to shove her behind me, block their view of her with my bigger body, and protect her, especially when I hear the smile in her voice and know it's forced. I want to hear what she sounds like when she's truly happy, what her smile looks like when it isn't strained and her pretty blue eyes aren't darkened by worry.

"What the hell is this, Jenna?" a man with more jowls than an English Bulldog barks at her. "What shit are you trying to pull now?"

"Good morning, Mr Thorne," she says pleasantly to the fat fuck sneering down at us. "I assume you're talking about my latest upgrades?"

"Upgrade? You call that ugly mess an upgrade?"

Ugly? You haven't seen ugly yet, you piece of shit.

"What you call ugly," Jenna begins, her voice bristling with anger—*that's my girl*—"I call ruggedly handsome."

My God, I want this woman. I want to wrap her in my arms and never let her go. When was the last time someone stood up for me? Even over something as simple as calling me names? I'm the protector. I'm the officer in charge. It's my job to stand up for others. And yet here's this small but fierce woman standing up for a brute like me. *Amazing.*

My mind is made up. When I get her the fuck out of here, I'm making her mine.

I'm keeping her.

One of the other suits pipes up. "Is it wearing one of our security uniforms?"

"Yes it is," she replies, offering no further explanation as she turns towards me. "As you can see, I've broadened the shoulders and expanded the chest, and—"

"It's ugly, Jenna," Fatty says again. "We don't sell ugly."

"Beauty is in the eye of the beholder, Mr Thorne," she snaps, turning to face the overgrown toad, "and I happen to find his new countenance *very* appealing, as will many of our clients."

"Our clients expect perfection," Thorne says, his tone condescending like he's explaining himself to a simple-minded child. "We sell the fantasy women want, and our research tells us what they want is a man with a six-pack, the face of a god, and a dick bigger than their husband's."

Jenna snorts derisively, which only angers Fatty more. "Yes, but not all fantasies are the same," she argues, "and I still maintain your research isn't broad enough. We're selling these sex-bots to women who can get whatever they want, whenever they want it. They can get men with six-packs and pretty faces and big dicks at a snap of their fingers. What they can't get is something a little rougher around the edges." She takes a breath. "Don't discount the working-man fantasy. The tradesman working in their home, the construction worker they pass on the street, the bodyguard protecting them. Women like a man who's good with his hands, someone who isn't afraid to get a little dirty. A beast to go with their beauty, if you will."

Thorne's mouth thins and he sniffs disdainfully, but he doesn't immediately shoot down Jenna's idea either. After a moment, he says, "Fine. I'll allow it. But if it doesn't yield results equal to or better than the original B.O.B., I'll personally see it thrown in the incinerator. Understand?"

Jenna nods once and smiles tightly. "Absolutely. If he doesn't blow my socks off, I'll even help you throw him in."

Damn, she is good. If I wasn't in on the con, I'd believe her.

My chest swells with pride, and it takes all my years of training to rein in my need to sweep her off her feet and spin her around, which is just plain crazy. But no more crazy than anything else that's happened today.

Is it possible to fall head over heels for a woman you just met? Obviously there's a physical attraction between us. The way she explored my chest earlier was anything but scientific. And don't even get me started on her reaction to seeing my cock. But in less time than it takes most people to drink a cup of coffee, Jenna has shown herself to be tough, a fighter, a survivor. But she's also vulnerable, sweet, and fiercely intelligent.

Could a woman like her ever want a man like me? A career soldier pushing fifty?

"As I was saying," Jenna continued, "I've widened the shoulders and expanded the chest to create a stronger-looking yet less defined physique, and given him a more rugged facial structure by squaring the jaw and shortening the hair. As usual, he's programmed with a variety of sexual commands and comes with the basic array of attachments, which can, of course, be customised for an additional price."

One of the other suits made an impatient noise and checked his watch. "Dr Johnson, your creative endeavours aside, what makes this bot different from the ones we already offer? Your brief, however vague, suggested you'd be showing us something more than a modified body and an unpleasant face."

"My brief. Of course." Jenna's tight smile returns. "I was just coming to that."

When she said "coming", two of the men who'd been leering at her snickered. *Wankers.*

But my girl soldiers on. "The upgrades I alluded to in the brief involved modifying the software to make B.O.B. more... spontaneous. It's something I've had my team working on for months, and I think you'll be pleasantly surprised." She pauses for effect. "I've added a random generator to his programming."

"Explain," Thorne demands.

"As you know, B.O.B. is the most advanced and dexterous bot in the world, capable of moving around as easily as a real human body does, and comes programmed with dozens of sexual positions and techniques, including kissing and cunnilingus. But the extent to which he can use his programming relies on the user giving specific commands in regard to what position she desires, and how long she wants sex to last.

"For example, the user would use commands like 'missionary position' or 'doggy style' to tell the bot what she wanted, along with a limit set either by time or the number of orgasms she desires before the session ends. With the random generator, the user can give commands such as 'seduce me' or 'make love to me' or 'fuck me hard', and instead of only one sexual position, the generator will randomly choose from a preset selection of several positions, creating spontaneity and making the overall sexual experience for the user more satisfying."

"And she can still choose the number of orgasms?" says one of the women in a suit, her gaze roaming over me as her hand goes to the base of her throat, much like Jenna's had earlier. I fight to keep the grin from my face, knowing full well she's picking up what Jenna is laying down.

"Of course," Jenna replies.

"Enough talking," Thorne grumbles. "Get on with the demonstration. I have more important things to do than stand around here all day watching you get your rocks off."

Yeah, like this whole set-up was Jenna's decision, you fat fuck.

Jenna turns to me, her jaw tight, her gaze focused. She swallows and says, "B.O.B., I want you to make love to me."

"As you wish, Jenna," I reply, keeping my voice stiff— robotic—just as my girl had instructed.

Besides the initial response, and a "You're welcome" when we finish, Jenna informed me the bots don't talk during sex, which suits me fine. I have much better uses for my mouth, especially when she unbuttons her lab coat and slips it off her shoulders, letting it pool on the floor by her feet.

I swallow hard at my first good look at her naked body. When she'd ripped her tank top off and I'd covered her up, I'd tried to avoid looking at her. Yes, I'd fantasised about the feel of my tongue on her nipples and sinking my cock deep inside her, but she'd looked so vulnerable in that moment. Ogling her then would have been the wrong thing to do.

But not now.

Now she's all mine to do with as I will. She wants me to make love to her? I am definitely here for that. I'd planned on making her mine once I got her out of here, but nothing says I can't start making her mine right now.

Chapter Six

J*enna*

REMUS REACHES BEHIND HIM, grabs the collar of his undershirt, and pulls it over his head, tossing it to the floor with my lab coat. I hear the women in the observation room gasp and coo their appreciation at the revelation of his strong chest, the thick slab of muscle giving true meaning to the term "beefcake".

Yummy.

Again my mouth pools with saliva, only this time there's nothing stopping me from leaning forwards and taking his nipple between my lips. But a quick lick is all I dare. Our aim is to get out of here as quickly and as alive as possible, and that means skipping the foreplay and getting down to business.

Two orgasms. That's all they need to see to be satisfied my new B.O.B. has what it takes to make them all lots and lots of money, and as primed as I am right now, I'm confident the demonstration will be over soon and Remus and I can get the hell out of here.

I flick my tongue over Remus's nipple and he shivers, but not too noticeably, thank goodness. While my bots can detect fluctuations in temperature—like a hot tongue pressed against a cold nipple—they don't react to them. Yet. It's something I'm working on.

But as quickly as that thought enters my mind, it leaves again, chased away by the feel of Remus's calloused hands cupping my face and tilting it upwards as his descends.

Fun fact! If you're ever curious about the size of a man's cock, look at his hands. A Korean study years ago concluded finger length was a much better indicator of a man's size than his feet.

And Remus has huge hands, with long, thick fingers.

Fingers that hold me in place as he angles his mouth over mine, and oh my *God*.

Real lips.

Real, firm, warm masculine lips are touching mine for the first time in years. Kissing me. And a real, slick tongue is pressing against them, asking for more than this chaste taste of bliss.

I eagerly open up to him and unashamedly whimper as his tongue brushes against mine, deepening the kiss and stealing my breath away. It only takes a moment for my libido to kick into high gear, and as Remus plunges his tongue in and out of my mouth in the most magnificently frenzied kiss, my hands fall to the waistband of his trousers.

With a flick of my wrist, I pop open the button and slide the zipper down, revelling in the purr of the metal teeth as they separate and reveal the hard, heavy weight of Remus's cock pressing against his cotton briefs. I swallow his soft moan and feel his body shudder as I slide my hand inside his underwear and ease him free of the fabric. When he pulls back from our kiss, I don't need to say a word.

The colonel is in control.

We didn't plan anything before the demonstration, didn't choose which positions we would use. I simply told him about the random generator idea and assured him I was on company-mandated birth control. Not that I needed it. In the three years I'd been held here, I'd never desired any of the men I worked with, neither scientist nor security guard. Remus promised me he hadn't been with anyone since his last physical. Either way, we don't have any condoms— robots don't exactly need them—so what choice do we have?

Remus stares down at me, a sly smile on his handsome face as he reaches between my legs and slips one strong finger through the slick folds of my pussy. My knees threaten to give out at the luxurious touch. How long has it been? How long since I was touched so intimately by a man? Caressed and teased and tormented the way Remus torments me now?

As good as I am at what I do, my bots just can't complete with a man like him.

I roll my lips between my teeth to keep from embarrassing myself, but with a gentle push, my lover enters my body and slowly thrusts in and out, his finger imitating the movement of his tongue in my mouth only moments ago. Imitating what he'll do when his cock replaces his finger in a few moments more.

Panting, I grip his forearms to hold myself up. Corded muscle shifts under my fingertips as he pulls out far enough to add a second finger to the first and thrusts back in, inch by glorious inch, then slowly circles his thumb around my clit. His actions are unhurried, deliberate, and so fucking good.

Is it possible to die from finger-fucking?

Because I am in Heaven. "Yes," I moan. "God, yes."

I'm so close to coming and he's barely touched me. I hear appreciative murmurs from behind the glass, both male and female alike. I try to block them out.

Fucking perverts.

Remember to stay on track. Remember the plan.

Have sex, buy time, escape.

Only I hadn't anticipated how horny for a real man I truly was, and now I'm afraid the time we buy with our little show may get all used up by the "have sex" part of the plan, because I don't want this to end.

It's then that Remus leans down, hiding his mouth from view while pretending to nuzzle my ear, and whispers, "Stop thinking so hard. Just let go. Let go and come for me, baby."

And then his mouth is on my neck, nibbling a path from below my earlobe to my jaw to my lips, stealing what little good sense I have left and devouring it like he can't get enough.

Seconds later, I snatch my mouth away from his and cry out my first orgasm.

My pussy clamps down on his fingers as my thighs clench around his hand. I feel the slickness on my skin, my arousal dripping all over Remus's fingers. Glancing up at him, I see his nostrils flare, and his eyes seem even darker than before, his gaze more intense.

His cock juts up between us, twitching and eager, the crown moist with his own arousal. He slips his hand out from between my legs and grabs my waist, then lifts my soft body as easily as he lifted the sex-bot and throws me down on the bed.

He doesn't even remove his pants before he's on me, just leaves them clinging to his narrow hips as he pins my arms above my head and starts licking and suckling my breasts. Taking my nipple in his mouth and drawing it upwards until the weight of my breast pulls it free from his lips. Over and over he does this. First one breast and then the other, he plies them with so much attention, and oh *fuck* that feels so good.

A real tongue. Real lips.

A real man.

Remus keeps most of his weight off me as he tortures my nipples into tight, reddened peaks, but his hips rock against mine, forcing his hard cock to rub against my clit over and over, almost to the same rhythm he's applying to my breasts.

At this rate he won't even need to fuck me.

My body is so primed for his, so eager. My legs fall open of their own accord, and Remus pulls back farther than before, far enough that I feel the blunted tip of his cock press against the outside of my pussy. Slowly he enters my body, and I can't suppress my groan.

Remus is so big, bigger than any of the sex-bots I've demonstrated over the last three years. He's stretching me open and filling me up, forcing my back to arch and thrusting my nipples against the solid muscle of his chest, abrading the overly sensitised buds until I'm fairly screaming with the ecstasy of it all.

True to my command, he goes slow, makes love to me. Thrusts into me with a languid rolling motion of his hips that near drives me crazy with wanting. Especially when he nuzzles the base of my throat and licks and nips at me, tormenting my erogenous zones with a precise gentleness that makes me weep.

It's too much. He's too much.

It feels so good.

I feel so lost.

And then he's whispering in my ear again, careful not to be seen by our observers. "Come for me, baby. Cry for me. Let me see you lose control."

He releases my wrists and lowers himself onto his forearms, pressing down on my body. In a flurry of desperation, I wrap my arms around his neck and my legs around his hips. I hold him as close as I can while he continues tormenting me with his slow thrusts and gentle caresses. And yes, I let the tears come.

I let them flood down my cheeks and release all the fear and hate and frustration, the longing and the loneliness. Three years' worth of sadness spills from my eyes until laughter bubbles up from within me and chases those tears away, replacing them with fresh tears. Tears of happiness. Tears of joy.

"That's my girl," Remus whispers, then thrusts harder, deeper, pushes himself up on his strong arms and takes me. Fucks me with his powerful hips until I'm screaming my second release.

As soon as my body stops shuddering through my orgasm, Remus withdraws and sits on the end of the bed, his cock still hard and glistening with my come, his hands resting on his thighs.

Right. He's a sex-bot. I'd almost forgotten.

Grabbing my lab coat, I quickly cover myself again before standing up and facing the group in the observation room. Most of the men have hard-ons. One of the women asks if she can bum a cigarette.

Mr Thorne, the fat pig, stares at me for a long moment in absolute silence, then says, "Fine. I won't toss it in the incinerator. But I want a full diagnostic report on my desk first thing Monday morning." Then he turns on his heel and leaves the room.

I let out a sigh of relief as the panel slowly slides down, hiding the observation window. Remus groans as if in pain, then flops back on the bed.

I rush to his side. "What's wrong?"

He doesn't move, just stares at the ceiling. "Need to come. Balls ready to explode."

Smirking at his robot voice, I lower myself to my knees in front of him and take his rock-hard cock in my hands. "Lucky for you the doctor is in." Leaning forwards, I take Remus in my mouth, tasting the sweet and salty combination of his pre-come mixed with my arousal still slick on his skin.

"Baby," he moans, his hands coming up to cup the back of my head and fist in my hair, guiding me where he wants me.

He wasn't kidding when he said he was ready to explode. I'm just getting into my groove when his thighs stiffen beneath me and his hips thrust up, forcing more of his cock down my throat as he comes with a masculine grunt, followed by a long, heavy sigh.

When I pull back, he sits up and smiles down at me, kneeling between his thighs. He strokes my cheek, those strong, gentle fingers smelling faintly like my pussy. "Did you swallow every drop?"

I nod and he reaches for me, pulls me into his lap. "Fuck, baby. Such a good girl." Then he kisses me long and deep, his tongue sweeping through my mouth like a hurricane of need.

I'm breathing hard when he pulls back, and my head swims with renewed arousal, but we have more pressing issues to take care of first. "So, how are we getting out of here?"

Remus looks around my room, then lifts one brow. "I don't suppose you have any explosives lying around?"

I nibble his earlobe. "Nope, sorry. Fresh out." Then I wink at him. "But I do have everything we need to make some."

Remus grins and squeezes my arse. "Jesus, Jenna. I don't know what the fuck I did to deserve you, but you really are my kind of woman," he says, then reaches for his undershirt. "Let's burn this shithole to the ground."

Chapter Seven

J*enna*

"WILL you tell me your name now? Your real name?"

After creating the mother of all distractions with our homemade explosives, Remus smuggled me out of the building amidst the sea of panicking people and led me away from the facility. His men had been waiting for us near a hole they'd cut in the security fence, and if they were shocked to see a woman dressed in a white lab coat, a pair of pink flannel pyjama bottoms, and sneakers, they hadn't shown it.

A short hike into the bush brings us to their base camp, where Remus throws out a few short, sharp orders, hands over my backup drive for safekeeping, then leans back against one of the big black vehicles, his lips pinching together in a sly smirk. "You wouldn't believe me if I told you."

I tilt my head and stare up at him, this beast of a man who put his life on the line to save mine. "Try me," I say and slide my hands over his firm chest, revelling in the feel of all that strength. I can't wait to get him naked again. Just the two of us this time, though. No more audience. No more perverted fat fuck-face. No more *demonstrations*.

Just me and Remus and sweet, hot sexy-times.

Wrapping his arms around my waist, he slides one hand down to squeeze my arse—he *really* likes my arse—then sighs and chuckles. "Fine. But don't say I didn't warn you." He hooks a knuckle under my chin and forces me to lift my gaze to his. I want to drown in the dark pools of his eyes. "My name, my *real* name, is Colonel Robert Morgan," he says. "But everyone calls me Bob."

Snapped out of my daydream, I stare at him, dumbfounded. "Bob? Your name... is Bob?" I shake my head, then let loose a hesitant laugh. He must be kidding. "You're right. I don't believe you."

Warm, firm, smiling lips crash against mine, coaxing mine to open wide enough for his silken tongue to slip between them and subdue any lingering doubts. "It's true, I promise," Remus whispers, leaning his forehead against mine. "And you know I keep my promises."

I do, don't I? From rescuing me to rocking my world, Remus has done everything he said he would, and all with a cocky grin and an air of command that makes my toes curl and my panties wet.

"Colonel, we need to go." A soldier dressed all in black opens the rear door to the waiting SUV.

Remus takes my hand and helps me climb into the back seat.

"What do we do now?" I ask, turning to peer through the rear window towards the carnage we created. Black plumes of smoke rise high into the sky, visible for miles, and sirens wail in the distance. I still can't believe no one is chasing us.

Remus curls one big hand around the nape of my neck and drags me closer, brushing his mouth over mine once more. "First we get you back to base for a debriefing," he says, then lowers his voice so his men don't hear him, "and then I take you back to my place for a de-*briefing*."

I giggle. I can't help myself, and I fucking *giggle*. "And how are you going to do that?" I whisper. "I'm not wearing any underwear."

The look on Remus's face is pure carnal predator, especially when he growls, "Fuck, baby. The things I'm gunna do to you when I get you home. You won't be able to walk for days."

He's so damn sexy. And sweet and corny, and I just want to rip his clothes off and—

"Ah, Colonel?" the soldier who held our door open says as he climbs into the driver seat. "Your earpiece is still active, sir. We can all hear you."

My giggle turns into full-blown laughter as Remus growls, "You're all fired." He rips the small plastic device out of his ear and tosses it in the front seat of the vehicle. "Get us out of here," he orders the driver. Then he turns to me and says, "Before we take this too far, I have to ask you something."

My mouth runs dry and I swallow hard at Remus's suddenly serious tone, but I nod, trusting him. He got us this far. "Okay. Ask me."

He takes a breath like he's about to ask me the most important thing in the world, then slowly lets it out. "Okay. So here it is. Cats... or dogs?"

I start to laugh until I see the small frown creasing his

brow. He's serious. *Okay, then.* After clearing my throat, I straighten my posture and tell him, "Cats. Definitely cats. Dogs are too needy."

My heart thunders in my chest as I await his verdict, and inside my head the words *Please be a cat person, please be a cat person, please be a cat person* are running on an infinite loop.

Then Remus grins, slow and sensual, and reaches for me again. "It's like you were fucking made for me, woman."

"And you were made for me, only better."

He cocks one brow. "Better? How so?"

I grin and slide my hand south, cup his cock through his trousers and feel it jump at my touch, feel it harden under my palm. "No batteries required to operate this boyfriend."

Matching my grin, he brushes his lips over mine. "Nope. This Bob runs on caffeine, chaos and cuss words."

Three of my favourite things. "Promise?" I murmur between teasing kisses.

"I promise, baby," he whispers back, and I snuggle against his chest. Warm. Safe. And horny as fuck. But not alone. Not anymore.

Not when I have my very own Bob.

TYING THE KNOT

For Alicia, thanks for making the dreaded day job way more fun than it had any right to be.

Chapter One

A *lly*

UN-FUCKING-BELIEVABLE.

My first night in town and my BFF bails on me. Not that I can be mad at her for it. She's an ER nurse and volunteered to do a double shift to help out with the heavier-than-usual traffic coming through the hospital doors at this particular time of year.

The time being January, and the particularity being the Tamworth Country Music Festival, when the population of the town swells to five times its usual size or more, and the propensity for people to wind up in the ER is in direct correlation with how much they've had to drink and whatever stupid thing they did after yelling at their mate to "Hold my beer."

So all of that just means I'm now sitting in a pub, drinking whisky... *alone*.

And the sharks have started to circle.

And by sharks, I mean cowboy wannabes.

These guys stick out like a sore thumb in their unscuffed boots and ostentatious belt buckles, jeans that are just a little too blue and Akubras straight from the saddlery, their pristine condition a dead giveaway their owners wouldn't know the arse end of a horse if it shit on their shoes.

Right now there are two of these morons trying to draw me into conversation, full of looking-to-get-laid swagger and not taking no for an answer. I've tried all the usual tricks to dissuade them, all the things women say to politely decline the advances of some random twat who may or may not turn out to be a serial killer.

"No."

"No, thank you."

"No, I don't want you to buy me a drink."

"Sorry, but I'm waiting for my boyfriend."

"Yes, my boyfriend is real."

"No, I don't want to save a horse and ride a cowboy."

"No, I'm not a lesbian."

All the shit women say while actively looking for ways to hobble the arsehole so we can make a clean getaway. But after driving for seven and a half hours to get here, then being ditched by my bestie, then dealing with these idiots, I'm no longer feeling very polite.

I raise my voice. "What part of *no* do you fuck-knuckles not understand? How many times do I have to say it before you get the fucking hint and back the fuck off? Jesus *fucking* Christ!"

Moron One and Moron Two stare at me like I've just sprouted a second head, and maybe I have. The Anti-Ally. That part of me that explodes outwards when confronted with arseholes either too clueless to realise they're making women uncomfortable or too selfish to care.

Then, just because I'm me and it couldn't end there, Moron Three joins the party.

"Ah, excuse me," he says loud enough to be heard over the din of the pub.

But before he can get in another word, I go on the attack.

"Oh, for fuck's sake. All I want to do is listen to music, sip whisky, and be left alone. Is that really so much to fucking ask?"

Morons One and Two exchange a sidelong glance, then slowly—*finally*—back away from the crazy lady. But Moron Three folds his thick arms across his sizeable chest, stares down at me, and grins. He fucking *grins* at me, and then an even weirder thing happens.

The anger burning in my chest stalls, then arrows downwards, morphing into a different kind of heat low in my belly, lower even than that.

Maybe it's the warmth and humour shining in the depths of his dark brown eyes, or maybe it's the way his sinful lips kick up in one corner that makes my mind nose-dive into the gutter, imagining all the naughty things I want him to do to me with his mouth. Whatever it is, I don't expect what he says next.

"Trinity said you had a mouth on you." He chuckles. "I guess she wasn't kidding."

I narrow my eyes on the newcomer, my lust momentarily forgotten as all my senses go back on alert. "Who are you, and how do you know Trinity?"

His grin broadens, and he nods ever so slightly, pinches the brim of his hat. "I'm Kade, her cousin. She said she tried calling to let you know I was coming to your rescue. You might want to check your phone."

Keeping one eye on my best friend's not unattractive alleged cousin, I fish my phone out of my handbag and see I have four missed calls, two voice messages, and one text. Pressing the phone to my ear, I try to listen to the voice messages, but the noise in the pub is ceaseless and the most I can make out is Trinity's voice saying, "...Ally... my cousin... you don't... Kade's like... fuck... the morning."

Okay.... Obviously I'm going to have to listen to that again later.

When I open the text message, a photo of Moron Three pops up, smouldering dark gaze, devilish grin and all, confirming he is who he says he is. Trinity's cousin.

Kade.

My rescuer, apparently.

Tucking my phone back in my bag, I let my gaze slide from the top of his worn but cared-for Akubra, down the front of his checkered cotton shirt, faded blue jeans, sensible belt buckle and polished yet well-used work boots.

Kade is definitely not a wannabe cowboy.

He's the real deal.

When I drag my gaze back to his, he has one brow cocked, and his grin has bloomed into a full-on panty-melting, making-me-weak-at-the-knees smile.

Holding his hands out to his sides, he says, "Do I pass muster, or would you like me to turn around so you can check out my arse?" Even through the noise in the increasingly crowded pub, Kade's deep voice carries. All the way to every single one of my sex receptors.

My nipples tighten. My clit pulses. My pussy grows wet, and my thighs clench around the emptiness between them, hoping, wishing Kade will step up and fill the void.

Please God, yes.

I haven't had sex in a while. Not since my loser ex decided he needed to be a "lone wolf" and ended our relationship. Seeing as he started banging anyone with two legs and a vagina the day after he dumped me, I assumed lone wolf was code for "I want to fuck other women and not feel like a dick about it."

Douchebag.

But what pisses me off the most is how deeply he made me doubt myself. I mean, I spent most of my twenties working to become the positive, confident woman I am today, so the fact one sorry excuse for a man could inflict such a massive dent in my self-esteem is *really* annoying. But maybe, just maybe, it's time to buff that dent out.

As I look my fill of the big man standing before me, I think I know exactly who to ask for a damn good buffing.

Mirroring Kade's grin, I ask, "Do you wanna get out of here?"

His eyes widen for just a moment, and I don't miss the way his gaze slides down my body and back again, checking me out the way I did him. By the time his eyes meet mine again, they're hooded, almost predatory, and he growls, "Abso-fucking-lutely."

Resting his hand on the small of my back, Kade guides me through the sea of bodies and back towards the entrance. The heat from his palm burns me through my T-shirt, and by the time we hit the street, I feel like I'm on fire. The air outside is muggy, like a storm's brewing, but it's cooler than the oppressive heat of the pub, and I take a much-needed breath.

What the hell am I doing?

"Did you drive in or walk?" Kade says, steering me

down the street, away from the pub and the crowd milling around outside.

"Walked." My voice is soft, subdued by the enormity of what I'm about to do. I don't usually jump into bed with strange men. That's just not who I am. As a sexual submissive, I need to know a man, know I can trust him before I let him anywhere near my body.

But I'm sick of always being alone, and *who I am* is getting me nowhere right now.

So maybe it's time to be someone else.

"I'm staying at that boutique hotel just down the street," I add, not so subtly hinting at the close proximity of an available bed.

Kade smiles down at me, and my knees actually wobble, but just as he opens his mouth to reply, a swarm of loud drunken women wearing miniature pink cowboy hats and belting out Dolly Parton's "Jolene" bustles past us. They knock me sideways and my knees give out completely. But before I get the chance to swear at them for being rude, a thick arm wraps around my waist, and suddenly I'm nestled against a hard body and—*sweet Jesus!*—an even harder cock.

"Are you all right?" Kade's concern melts the last of my indignation.

I swallow hard. "Uh-huh."

"Good," he says, and I feel the press of his lips against my ear. "Now, the way I see it, sweetheart, we have three options."

"Oh?" I really want to wiggle my butt against his erection, but when he tightens his grip, I instinctively hold still and wait.

Apparently my submissive side is eager to please him.

"One, I walk you back to your hotel room and we say goodnight."

I shrug and play it cool, attempting to calm my raging heartbeat. "Meh. What else you got?"

"Two, we find someplace we can eat and talk for a few hours, and then I walk you back to your hotel room and we say goodnight."

"Hmm, not that I'm not tempted, but unless you booked a table two weeks ago, I doubt we're eating out tonight. Besides,"—I reach back and slide my hands up Kade's muscular thighs, then turn my head to whisper over my shoulder—"it's not food I'm hungry for."

Kade's grin is wide and wicked. "That just leaves option three," he says, his voice a velvety purr.

"Oh? And what's option three?"

"I take you back to my place, tie you up, and fuck you so goddamn hard you forget your own name."

My whole body shivers with anticipation—a feeling completely at odds with the heated throbbing between my thighs—and I suck down an excited breath.

Kade chuckles. "Option three it is, then."

Chapter Two

K *ade*

WHEN MY COUSIN rang me in a panic and asked me to entertain her friend because she'd had to ditch her at the last minute for work, I'd grumbled at her about owing me one. Then I'd done what family does: changed into my nicer jeans and a clean shirt, grabbed my hat, and headed into town.

Trinity had texted me the name of the pub, a photograph, and a brief description of her friend—tall, angry, swears like a soldier—so it wasn't difficult to find the woman.

The photo didn't do her justice, but the description was spot on.

Her anger was glorious, and the mouth on her... *fuck*. My cock has throbbed with need from the moment I heard her chewing out those fuckwit townies playing at dress-ups.

Wearing tight blue jeans and a pink T-shirt with "Spurs and Bling, It's a Cowgirl Thing" printed across her perfect tits in scrolling silver lettering, it was easy to see why she'd attracted the attention of said fuckwit townies. But I'm guessing that's all they saw, long legs and a nice rack. They weren't the sort to appreciate a strong woman like Ally, as they'd proven at the first hint of her temper when they'd tucked tail and run.

Me? I like strong.

I like smart and confident and independent. I like a woman who knows what she wants and what she doesn't. And it was pretty damn obvious to me from the moment I saw her that what those idiots were offering was nothing she wanted.

Definitely nothing she needed.

And it hadn't taken me long to figure out what that was either.

Ally revealed her hand when she let me lead her out of the pub, and again when that hen party barged past us on the footpath, knocking her into me.

Not once did she try to swat my hands away as I'd wrapped them around her body, or swear at me like she had with everyone else. It was almost like her submissive nature had sensed my dominant one, and Ally had settled against me like a contented cat, held still, and let me push my rock-hard erection against her soft arse as I kissed the shell of her ear and murmured my salacious suggestions.

She was eager for me too. She wouldn't have volunteered the whereabouts of her accommodation so easily otherwise. Or touched my thighs, or blatantly told me she was hungry for something other than food.

Suddenly I'm thinking it might be me owing Trinity a favour and not the other way around.

"So where's this place of yours, then?" Ally asks as we climb into my car.

"I own a ten-acre stretch in the next town over. It's only a fifteen-minute drive." Which is fifteen minutes too many that I'm not inside this woman. Sure, I could've taken her back to her hotel and been balls deep already, but I have a hunch my Ally-Cat is a screamer, and I don't want anything inhibiting her tonight. Taking her to my place, where my nearest neighbour is almost a kilometre away, should allow her the freedom to be herself.

Me too.

After a quick stop to buy condoms, we fill the time with idle chit-chat, that sort of nervous talk two people engage in when they're counting down the minutes to showtime and, through no fault of their own, have to keep their hands to themselves. I tell her I breed horses; she informs me she owns a cat. I invite her to go riding while she's visiting; she admits she's never ridden a horse before.

Then, for some completely unfathomable reason, I tell her my cousin thinks I need a wife.

And just as I pull up in front of my house, Ally tells me she's *very* single.

I cut the engine and we both sit there, silently staring out the windscreen, the air between us thick with expectation. Then the storm that's been threatening all afternoon cracks open the sky and fat droplets of rain start falling, hitting the car with a rhythmic *thud, thud, thud,* quickly increasing in speed and volume until it's almost deafening.

Ally flashes a grin and yells over the noise, "Race you!" Then she's out of the car and running towards the house, undaunted by the deluge of water soaking her to the bone.

It takes mere seconds for me to catch her on the stairs, wrap my arm around her waist, and lift her off her feet. I pin her to my front door, sopping wet and laughing, and kiss the ever-loving hell out of her.

When I take Ally's mouth, the taste of smooth whisky explodes across my tongue, and suddenly I'm dying of thirst. I can't get enough of her. But my girl starts to shiver as the cold and the wet overtake her lust, and I have to take care of her first.

"Let's get inside and get out of these clothes," I murmur against her lips.

She fists her hands in my shirtfront and offers me a coy little smile. "I thought you'd never ask."

As soon as the door is open, I toss Ally over my shoulder and head straight for the lounge room. "Strip," I command, putting the wriggling woman back on her feet. "I'll get a fire going."

Ally toes off her boots. "In the middle of summer?" Her sweet voice holds a teasing lilt, and I can't wait to hear it hitch with passion. Hear her moan.

Make her beg.

"That storm isn't going anywhere anytime soon, Ally-Cat. And your skin is like ice. A fire will take the chill off. Now do as you're told and strip off those wet clothes."

She grins at me, then peels her sodden T-shirt over her head, dropping it to the timber floor with a wet *slap*. "Yes, Sir."

Ignoring the rush of lust filling my veins at the sound of her calling me "Sir", I stare at the mess on my floor before raising my unimpressed gaze to her defiant one. "Hmm... maybe I should call you Ally-Brat."

My unrepentant girl laughs, but when I cock one brow and fold my arms across my chest, she bites her lip and drops her gaze, and my dick hammers at my zipper, demanding release from its denim prison.

But first we need to get warm—dry, at the very least—so I crouch down and make short work of lighting a fire in the hearth. By the time I'm done, Ally is down to her underwear and busying herself draping clothes over chairs.

I take a moment to enjoy the view, then hang my hat and toe off my boots, setting them near the fire. I strip my shirt off next and hand it to Ally to hang up while I fetch us some towels and the quilt off my bed.

When I return, I find Ally in front of the fire, wringing water from her long blonde hair, shivering as it trickles down her back. I cast aside the blanket and pull her into my arms, wrap a towel around her shoulders, and begin drying her.

"I must look like a drowned rat," she murmurs, her gaze diverted and her mouth pulling south at the corners. "Not exactly sexy."

Not exactly sexy? Fuck that.

I drop the towel and unfasten my jeans, releasing my cock—my very hard, very eager cock. "I beg to differ."

Ally drops her gaze, then drops her jaw, and I'd be lying if I said I'm not preening just a little bit. Especially when she sinks her teeth into her bottom lip and whimpers.

I know I'm a big man. At six foot four, I'm taller than the average bloke, a little broader in the shoulders and thicker through the middle. I have big hands, big feet and... well, you know what they say about men with big feet.

But with greying hair, mud brown eyes, and a nose I've broken more times than I can remember, I'm not winning any beauty contests either, so the last thing I want is Ally thinking she doesn't measure up.

Threading my fingers through her still damp hair, I push it away from her face, stare deep into her gorgeous blue eyes, and hide my smile. "You are the sexiest drowned rat I've ever seen."

A burst of laughter escapes her, and I let loose my grin, then take her mouth in a slow and torturous kiss.

Fuck, she tastes good, and I don't just mean the whisky lingering on her tongue. Ally is heat and lust, sex and longing and need.

Craving.

Or maybe that's me.

"Beautiful."

"Kade," she moans, the sound hitting me right in my balls. I feel her hands on my hips, urging my jeans down over my arse and thighs, and I growl my approval.

I don't remember the last time I was with any woman, let alone one as beautiful as Ally. Sure, she's tall and she has nice tits, but *fuck*, there's something about her that makes me want to wrap her up and keep her. Something vulnerable in the depths of her eyes, something that begs me to keep her safe.

It's the way she touches me, like she's exploring uncharted territory, learning every inch of my body the way I long to learn about hers.

Reaching behind her, I unclasp her bra, then tug it free and cup her breasts. Her skin is pale and still slightly damp, but her nipples respond to my touch, hardening against my palms, two perfect pink peaks begging for attention.

Breaking away from our kiss, I trail my lips along her jaw and down her throat, across her shoulder, along her collarbone and down the centre of her chest.

But before I take one more liberty, I ask, "What's your safe word, Ally?"

Because I know she has one.

Her eyes flutter open and she audibly swallows, then confirms my suspicions. "Banana bread."

I can't disguise my grin. "Seriously?"

Ally shrugs. "What? I hate banana bread. It's not something I'm likely to blurt out for no reason."

"Good point. Banana bread it is. Now come here, little cat."

Her smile is blinding, and as I bend and take her breast in my mouth, her quick gasp and sultry moan are like music to my ears. And when I pinch her nipple between my teeth and gently tug on it, I feel her claws dig into my shoulders like she's hanging on for dear life, determined not to fall.

"That feels so fucking good." Her voice is barely a whisper, escaping her mouth on a shuddering breath. I continue sucking and biting her breasts, massaging and plumping them. Then I squeeze them, increasing the pressure until her mouth falls open and her eyes roll back and her keening cry fills the room. "Kade!"

I press my lips to her ear and snarl, "Bend over the fucking couch."

I pull back to enjoy her whimper, revel in the unrestrained lust I see written across her face, in the blush of colour staining her cheeks and the slight parting of her lips as she whispers, "Yes, Sir."

Chapter Three

In-fucking-credible!

Thank you, Trinity, for working overtime.

Thank you, douchebag ex, for dumping my arse.

And thank you, powers that be, for sending Kade to my rescue tonight, because *damn*, if this man fucks as well as he kisses, then stick a fork in me because I am done.

Ruined for all other men.

Kade is sexy as fuck. A silver fox with rakish good looks, a rich, velvety voice and a strong, thick body. And I can't wait to feel that monster he calls a cock deep inside me. Stretching me open.

I turn to face the couch and bend at the waist as instructed, bracing my hands on the seat cushions. "Like this?"

"Exactly like that. Good girl," Kade says, his praise

sending warmth of another kind careening through me, making me happy. I look over my shoulder in time to see him kick off his jeans and realise he's not wearing any underwear. Somehow, I'd missed that tiny detail when I was gawking at his enormous dick. "Eyes front, sweetheart."

"Yes, Sir."

I don't know where this submissive side of me comes from—it's just always sort of been there—but I do know finding someone who understands, someone who gets it and doesn't make fun or ridicule or take advantage is as rare as fucking hen's teeth.

Kade gets it, he understands, and I trust he won't take advantage. I trust him, because I trust Trinity, because she knows and accepts me for what I am—a kinky bitch who loves being tied up, spanked, fucked and treated like a pet—and she would never hurt me. Would never send someone else to hurt me.

Kade strokes his big hands over my arse, and I can't help but clench up. Not out of fear, mind you, but anticipation. Will he spank me? Won't he? Will he rip my panties off with his teeth? A girl can hope.

"You have the cutest bum. So round. So soft." *Slap*. My arse jiggles, and I hear Kade groan. "So pliant."

My breath saws in and out of my lungs in short excited bursts. The slap on my arse didn't hurt, but it wasn't tentative either. Kade is just warming up.

Slap. His hand lands on the other cheek.

Slap, slap. My arse is starting to burn.

Slap, slap, slap, slap. My skin is tight and hot, my body needy. I arch my back and cry out. "More! Please, more."

"Beautiful," he murmurs, stroking his hands over me again, gently raking his fingernails over my sensitive flesh before slipping one hand between my legs, shifting my lacy underwear aside and spearing two fingers inside my cunt. My legs quiver, threatening to give out beneath me. Kade speaks again, his voice awed. "So pink. So pretty." One more *slap*. "So wet and so very fuckable."

Before I can respond, Kade hooks his fingers through my panties and slips them down my legs. Then I hear the crinkle of a condom wrapper, and suddenly the blunt head of his cock is prodding between my thighs. I stay facing forward as commanded, but I can't help the eager little wiggle in my hips as he lines up our bodies and slams home.

"Ally." Kade's voice is pure pleasure, and for a moment he doesn't move. Then he rocks his hips and begins that erotic slide of flesh on flesh, of sex. *Fucking*. "Ally," he groans again. "This is going to be quick and dirty, sweetheart. I haven't had a woman in a very long time and you're so fucking tight."

"Do it," I beg him. "Take me. Use me. I want this." I push back as he thrusts forwards. "I want you."

"My little Ally-Cat." He anchors himself to me with one hand tightening on my waist and the other fisting in my hair, pulling my head back like he's reining in a wilful horse. "I'm gunna make you scream."

Kade keeps his promise.

He fucks me hard and fast and hits every nerve ending along the way. I'm so wet I feel it slipping down my thighs, so desperate to come my fingers are ready to tear the couch cushions apart. And when he bottoms out inside me, when he slams his hips against my arse and shouts my name to the heavens, I scream in ecstasy.

I scream so goddamn loud. More than I think I ever have. I feel no inhibition with this man, no reason not to yell and scream and beg for more. Besides, we're in the middle of bloody nowhere with a storm raging all around us. Who's going to hear me?

When Kade pulls out, I collapse on the couch. His warm chuckle follows me. "I hope I didn't wear you out."

"Not a chance."

"Good girl." He strokes my cheek. "Wait here."

Kade disappears for a few minutes, then returns with a fresh erection and what looks like a length of satin rope. My interest piques.

"Stand up, little cat, and turn around."

I like Kade's pet name for me. Hell, I like a lot of things about this man. As I climb to my feet and face away from him again, I think about what he said earlier, how Trinity said he needs a wife.

And I told him I was available.

"Hands behind your back."

Kade's voice is rough and sexy, a deep masculine rumble I would happily listen to for as long as we both shall live.

He sweeps my hair over my shoulder and out of his way, then gathers my wrists in one large hand and wraps the satin cord around them, binding them securely.

"Our first time was over too fast for my liking, sweetheart." He presses a kiss to my shoulder, nuzzles against my neck. "This time will be slower. This time you don't come until I say so. Understand?"

"Yes, Sir."

"Good girl."

With one last slap on my tender arse, he positions us so he's sitting on the couch and I'm straddling his lap. I watch him roll a fresh condom over his huge erection—*sexy as fuck*—then gasp as he lifts me up like I weigh nothing at all, notches his cock against my pussy, and slides home.

"Oh my God!" If I thought Kade was big before, it's

nothing compared to what I think now. This new position, this new angle is... *everything*. I'm full to the point of pain, but it's a hurt I crave.

Wetness gushes from my body and we're not even moving. Then Kade cups my aching arse cheeks and slowly lifts me up and down and up and down, rolling his hips so the head of his cock strokes over my G-spot every fucking time. My head lolls back and his name escapes me on a moan. "Kade."

"I've got you, little cat. I've got you."

Yes you do.

I feel my orgasm building. I want to spill over the edge, but I also want Kade to control my pleasure. I want to hear his commanding voice giving me permission, want to feel his heated breath on my throat when he orders me to come.

I need a distraction. Something, anything to slow myself down. Like conversation. "Did Trinity really say... you need a wife?"

Kade chuckles and our bodies bounce together, edging me even closer to orgasm. Staring up at me with his gorgeous chocolate-coloured eyes and a broad grin, he says, "She did." He tilts his head to one side, his gaze growing shrewd. "You want the job?"

"Depends. What would the job... entail?" I'm struggling to breathe, every little thrust of his hips pushing the air from my lungs. "What do you want... in a wife?"

Breaking neither pace nor eye contact, Kade says, "Well, I like smart women. Strong, too. Beautiful." He moans and his eyelids shutter. "With blue eyes and long blonde hair. And a temper... she has to have a temper." His grin broadens. "And say 'fuck' a lot."

Barely restraining my smile of glee, I ask, "Is that all?"

"Nope. I want a submissive woman... sexually speaking.

One who loves... being spanked and tied up and fucked."
Then he looks away, like he's thinking. "Hmm... cooking
skills are advantageous but not necessary, and the big one,
obviously... oh, God," he groans and bucks up into me, his
breathing is as staggered as my own. "She must love riding
horses."

Now I look away and pretend to think, a ruse that
would have been more effective had my hands not been tied
behind my back. Tapping my finger against my chin really
would have sold it.

"What if she just loves riding a man,"—I gasp—"who's
hung like a horse?"

Kade chuckles again, and the rich sound vibrates down
through his body, then up through mine. "Where the fuck
have you been all my life?"

I shrug. "Queensland."

Kade picks up his pace, and I cry out, the delicious
sensations he's wringing from my body making me hungry
for more.

Our slow fuck full of tenderness turns brutal. Kade's
fingers dig into my hips as he works my body faster, slams us
together harder. Our conversation dissolves into grunts and
gasping, and what was languid and controlled is now a
frenzy of need and wanting.

My head falls back and my body shakes. I'm so close. So
fucking close. But I can't come yet. Not until Kade says so.

"Look at me, Ally." Kade's voice is barely a growl. So
guttural and demanding. "Don't you dare look away."

I nod my compliance as I return his molten gaze. My
body is hot, my skin beaded with sweat. Lightning crashes
outside, but it's the storm in my mind and in my heart that's
charging the air with electricity.

"Please, Sir. Please, I need to come."

Kade's eyes soften, and he cups my cheek. "Little cat, you beg so beautifully." He wraps that hand around my throat, restricts my breathing to the bare minimum needed to survive, then grits his teeth and snarls at me. "Come for me, Ally. Come now."

Tears stream down my cheeks as I scream my release. More intense than the last, my orgasm takes hold of me entirely and doesn't let go. Shakes me to my core.

Beneath me, Kade still bucks and writhes, thrusting up into me like a man possessed until his own roar of completion threatens to drown out the storm.

He lets go of my throat and I fall forwards on his chest, both of us sucking down much-needed air. Then I feel the quilt being dragged over the top of us and Kade's hands stroking my body, petting me and offering comfort.

When he finally speaks, his voice is warm but unsure, cautious. "Did I hurt you, little cat? Did I push you too hard?"

I shake my head and snuggle closer, burrowing against his chest. "I liked it. A lot."

His chest bounces with a chuckle and he plants a kiss on top of my head. "In that case, wanna do it again?"

I lift my gaze to his, let him see my smile, my eagerness. My submission. "Abso-*fucking*-lutely."

More from Jennie Kew

THE BENNETT'S BASTARDS SERIES

Third Time Lucky

This Time Around

His Own Heaven

The Viking Blues

Size Doesn't Matter (2022)

A Thousand Words (2023)

THE BRISBANE BACHELORS SERIES

Revenge and Redemption

Sacrifice and Seduction

AUDIOBOOKS

Revenge and Redemption

THE Q COLLECTION

No Rest For The Wicked

I Saw, I Conquered, I Came

Pushing Rope

Dirty Laundry

Santa Claus Is Coming

Carved In Stone

Battery Operated Boyfriend

Tying The Knot

Quirky: The Complete Q Collection

Acknowledgments

To my family for all their encouragement, their love and understanding, thank you for being you and for putting up with me being me, especially when deadlines are involved.

A special thank you to my crit partners, my cheer squad, my sisters-in-arms, Bec McMaster and Kylie Griffin. You always challenge me to be a better writer and I really couldn't do this without you. Thank you for keeping me sane...*ish*.

To my editor, Kristin Scearce, who accepts my weird writing style and quirky humour as canon and is still willing to work with me, you rock!

To Efthalia Pegios for translating Nadia's curse and for explaining how many ways you can interpret the word "cock" in Greek. Coffee is on me!

And finally to my readers, thank you for taking this journey with me, and for allowing me to share with you all the people and places who occupy my head and my heart. I hope you enjoy reading about them as much as I enjoy writing about them.

Meet the Author

Jennie has always enjoyed reading but never had aspirations of becoming a published author. At least not until a dance with death made her ask herself what she really wanted out of life, and she's been writing ever since.

When not writing stories about her imaginary friends, Jennie can usually be found reading a book, watching a movie or building stuff out of Lego. She lives in regional New South Wales with her husband, her husband's magnificent beard, and their small menagerie of furry companions.

www.jenniekew.com